I0546509

Amid A Crowd of Stars

"... And paced upon the mountains overhead,
And hid his face amid a crowd of stars."
William Butler Yeats, from <u>When You Are Old</u>, 1893

Copyright © 2025 by Joseph McConnell. All rights reserved. No part of this book may be used or reproduced in any manner whatsoever without written permission except in the case of brief quotations embodied in critical articles and reviews.
For permissions, contact the Author
ISBN 978-1-7377945-5-4

This is a work of fiction. All characters in this work are inventions, and they do not represent real people, living or otherwise.
"Amid a Crowd of Stars" is part of the final line of Yeat's poem, "When You Are Old." The poem is said to refer to Maud Gonne, who, it implies, will regret rejecting Yeats. Here, the reference is simply to two people who decide to accompany each other while bouncing madly around the universe.
This book is for Linda and our dog and for women anywhere whose plans and inclinations are threatened by authority.
Cover photo and design by the author.

Contents

Preface: An Old Question

They weren't visible with the naked eye. They were there, though, three of them at the moment, in stationary orbits. They'd been called shoe boxes - they were rectangular shapes, a dull metal color in most places., They had the approximate volume of a small office building. In the canon of human space creations, they were easily the least impressive-looking. But they were star-faring vehicles.

Two of them were training, research, and planning facilities, moving with the Earth, shifting to different places in orbit as the work required. The other one was, no matter how it looked, a Starship. Two more like it were away at the moment, visiting star systems elsewhere in the galaxy. Taken together, they all represented the most recent effort by humanity to flex its muscles, leave the home planet, and try to answer the old, old question: *What's out there?*

One: Older Women and Younger

The staff car slowed for a pedestrian couple. They were crossing the street as casually as people of student age tended to. "Come on, folks," the driver said. His passenger glanced up, then looked back down at her phone. She scrolled past messages from a range of people, mostly officials in the country's government, a few from elsewhere. One was the traditional *Have a good day, dear* from her partner. Another was from her superior officer, letting her know he'd be in a bit late.

She turned the phone off and looked up. They were almost at the building, a unique, unmistakable mass of 1970s concrete paranoia. It used to be a university administration center, slated for teardown; only the Separation saved it from destruction. The new government needed a headquarters for its national military police, and intelligence services, and this rectangular solid was a good match; she and her department occupied the top three floors.

"Was that actually a sun beam I just saw?" she asked the driver.

"Yes, Sir. We might see slightly less cold and damp today." He pronounced it "Coldendamp", as though it were a German or Austrian municipality. As for the "Sir" part, that was standard in the Republic's military. If you were speaking to someone of higher rank, you said "Sir," regardless of gender.

"Fine with me." The car turned into the parking lot. As the driver brought it to a stop, another person in uniform, a woman with a holstered sidearm, stepped up and opened the door. "Oh, come on, Andrea," the passenger said, " I can actually let myself out of a car, still."

"I know, General. But it makes me feel needed."

The passenger was General Eden Bienvenue Gorsky, Army of the Republic, Commanding the Intelligence Branch. She entered the building via a side door, opening onto a small elevator lobby. You needed one of a specific set of badges to get in and, once in, to make the elevators work; needless to say, hers did those things. She was mildly surprised that no one else was coming in the same way at this hour, but things weren't all that rigorous, at least in her command. Her people worked the hours that had to be worked, and the work wasn't the kind of thing that involved clock punching.

Clock punching, she thought as the lift went up. *What the hell does that mean?* The concept of an alarm clock, let alone a so-called time clock was nearly gone from the language. She'd heard it once or twice, but never had any real idea of it. The car stopped and the doors slid open; elevators had survived, clocks hadn't. *There's something profound, there*, she thought, *but I have no idea what it is. Oh, well.*

She walked four or five steps to a door with no sign on it, a device read a signal from another, smaller device built into her phone, and the door opened. Her eyes opened widely, and she took a step back.

"Good morning, General!" said thirty-eight people, standing around in the space beyond the door.

===

After a brief period of confusion and concern, setting aside the idea of a mutiny of some kind, and basically getting her act together, she allowed herself to be congratulated on thirty-five years of service in the Army of the Republic. Over those years, she'd served in all three of the Army's groups: the military, law enforcement, and, to put it bluntly, spying organizations. The groups were called branches: Field Branch, Security Branch, and Intelligence Branch. Gorsky had essentially invented the latter one, and for the last ten years, she'd commanded it.

Among those gathered to celebrate her tenure were her superior officer, General Phillip Hallstatt, and Gorsky's partner, Doctor Kristin Horstel. She and Gorsky had been together for decades, and Horstel had a key role in the civilian government; she was the Director of the Republic's Department of Education.

The country was formally called The Peninsular Republic. It was a young nation, just forty years old. Geographically, it was the two peninsulas, upper and lower, that used to comprise the US State of Michigan. Culturally, it wasn't particularly enthusiastic about medals and honors, but it could manage to dig up a symbol for occasions like this one. Everyone, in any part of the Army of the Republic, wore a small, square, hook-and-loop badge on their left breast-pocket flap, the color indicating rank. For Gorsky, that was bright red, meaning that she was a general in command of a Branch.

Today's little event was taking place because the Government had recently authorized a thirty-year-service symbol to go in the center of those badges. It was a small brass pin, and it said, naturally, "30." On the day the award was put into practice, there were already twenty-eight people of all ranks who qualified, including Gorsky, and they were being given their pins in alphabetical order, rather than highest to lowest. This was the kind of egalitarian ethos that the Republic liked to apply, and people had come to expect it.

General Hallstatt, the highest-ranking officer in the Army, stepped forward and handed Gorsky her decoration. "Thirty years, E. Time flies, doesn't it?"

"Thank you, General. I have to admit, I don't know how long *you've* been in. You must be close, though."

"I am, but I'm not quite there. Three years to go."

Gorsky's partner came up behind him and said "Move over, soldier. I get to put the pin on." She pulled the hook-and-loop square off, fastened the "30" pin on it, and patted it all back in place. "Now, then ... " She gave her partner a big hug, then stepped back and said "All hail the queen of snooping!" The group cheered in a sort of reserved, socialist way.

===

Later that afternoon, Horstel was back at the Department of Education building. Room 101 was a big room, one of the biggest conference rooms in the Government's collection of places to gather. Today, the people gathered in it were those concerned with the

Republic's educational programs and their definition, distribution, and teaching. The people present were DoE personnel, and they all had some responsibility for maintaining the courses and material related to a set of topics. A giant screen was displaying the phrase "The Starship Program Curriculum Update."

The team lead had been standing at a table at the front of the room, waiting for people to settle in. It was a small group, but using this particular conference space was a kind of signal. It said, *This is an important topic. Show up and pay attention.*

"Let's get started," the Program Lead said. "Director Horstel wants to kick off this round of updates, and here she is." Kristin stood up and walked to the table.

"Thanks, John. I want us to go back over this, from the start, because people join the department or transfer to the Starship program all the time, and we need to be sure that everybody's on the same page." She paused and looked around the group. "Now, you all know some of this initial stuff, and since it's historical, we're unlikely to change our class content all that much. But I want to be sure we at least review the basic points as we work through this update." The screen changed to say "No Contact."

"You've heard that, over and over. I sure have, and I hope the average student has, too. So this is the rock-bottom explanation, as it's been all along." The screen changed. It displayed the number *1,127,000*, followed by the word *dead*.

"Eighteen years ago, a private, for-profit space exploitation project brought back soil samples from a moon of Jupiter - Io, in fact. Because they did that, one million, one hundred and twenty-seven thousand people died from the bacteria that came with it. There are still eight people alive, carrying the disease and quarantined in the Australian outback. The executives and big investors of the company that brought it in are still in jail."

There was little reaction, although Kristin noticed a person in the second row brushing what might have been a tear off his cheek. She went on. "The horror of that grossly irresponsible action changed the world. As a result, three large groups of nations formed an alliance and agreed to mandate that all off-planet activity would be solely non-profit and Government-only. "

"So," she went on, "No rich guys go to Mars, nobody gets to mine anything, nobody gets to bring anything back. And half the world acts together to enforce it. The group is ... " The screen changed to display *EurAsiaNA*. "That's the European Union, the Chinese and their neighbors, and North America. We're a part of it, and we were able to add our concept that safety and comfort for the whole outweighs individual gain. The Starship program has endorsed that and included it in its charter. So that describes the underlying constraint for human movement off planet Earth. But ... ?" She looked around. An older man in the second row of seats raised a hand. "Go ahead, Frank," Horstel said.

"We still want to know ... " He paused. "... what's out there?"

"Exactly. You've heard my little speech before. Five or six times, at least. And here's the answer we've been providing as a starting point. The screen began echoing her words.

"Nine years ago, some really smart people figured out a way to get out of the solar system. ESSTC, *Extra-Solar-System-Travel-Capability*. These courses don't talk about how it works. That's for the Physics people. But it does work:" The screen began a series of images of blocky, rectangular structures, obviously outside a planetary atmosphere and presumably in orbit. "That, whether it looks like it or not, is a Starship."

"We - we as in humanity - have built Starships. Like that one. We can get off this rock and go out and look at other rocks. And get back again. Right now, we're doing it in just our own galaxy. And ..." The screen displayed *We don't bring things back*.

"The younger and more enthusiastic our students are, the more that constraint upsets them. But what we *can* do is go out and visit other solar systems, see if they have planets, and orbit around a few of them. We *image the hell out of 'em*, as a friend of mine says. And if that turns up interesting targets, we drop some highly sterile probes and surface rovers that can move around on the surface. We see what they see, and then we leave the hardware. On the ground or in orbit. We analyze, report and move on."

"Now," she said, "That usually brings up a fundamental question: What if we find something? Here's what the Director of the whole Program, speaking for all of the member nations, says about that." The screen said "Doctor Stephanie Leydon, PhD, Program Director." It began showing video of a woman, apparently in conversation with someone out of the picture. A voice said "What do you think these missions will find?"

The woman - Doctor Leydon - answered. "In the sense of your question, I don't. I don't think about what they'll find. I have no hypothesis regarding it. If you mean *Will they find microbes?* or *Will they find advanced civilizations?* I can't answer those questions. And the biggest question is *will they find life at all?* That's out of scope. It's not a question that *can* be answered. Because we don't even know what we mean by the word *life*. All our ideas are driven by what we see here. And if I expect anything at all, I expect them *not* to find a planet full of biped mammals, preparing to send up star ships to see if there's life anywhere else."

The interviewer, still off screen, said, "All right. But why are we doing it at all, then?"

"To answer the question, not i*s there life?* but *what is there?* And to tag that old book no one seems to read any more, *what then must we do?"*

Kristen let that sit for a moment. Then she said, "Here, what we must do is design the next release of our curriculum covering the Starship Programs, EurAsiaNA, and the educational path that a student might take in order to grow up and be a Starship sailor."

===

"What if she doesn't get it?"

"We're sorry, we're supportive, we hoped she would get it, it's a pity ... and if she wants to take a bit of a break, now, she's always welcome to come home. Spend some time here. Decide what comes next."

"And what if she *does*?"

"We're delighted for her. It's what she's wanted, now, for years, and we're so happy. We remind her that Liscannor is always home, any time she can ... get here. When she's not ... up there."

"All right. I ... will likely let you do most of that, then, either way. But ... oh, here we are!" Their phone screen lit up, showing a still image of a young woman, early thirties, perhaps, with shoulder length reddish-blonde hair and a neutral expression: Anna Martiné Grover's caller image.

The man who'd been asking the *what if* questions touched the screen. The image changed to a video version of itself. "Hello, dear heart," he said. His wife echoed him.

"Hello, hello," said Anna. She appeared to be controlling herself, initially, then broke into a smile. "I got it," she said.

"Well, wonderful! We're so happy for you! Aren't we, Stephen?"

"Of course, of course. Congratulations!"

"Will you have any time before ... before you go? To come home, I mean?"

Anna had anticipated that. "Yes," she said. "Probably a week or five days, at least. And I'd love to come. Maybe drive up to the Pollboy Lookout. I haven't seen the sea for ... ages. Or anything like a cliff."

"We do have cliffs here," said her Father. "And sea enough ..." He paused. "To look at." He'd meant to say "For any reasonable person," but cut himself off. *We're happy she's got what she was working for,* he thought. *Happy. Remember that.*

The conversation went on in that manner for another twenty minutes. Anna did most of the talking, describing the interviews, the testing, the medical exams. In the end, she'd realized that it had all been slightly perfunctory; the program had four open positions and, this particular quarter, three applicants. But she could sense the anxiety her parents were feeling, mixed with the pride, and she didn't want to diminish any of the latter. *I understand it, I guess. Having your daughter flung into space must be a little ... unsettling.*

When they said goodbye, the parties on both sides of the call felt a kind of relief. The parents had been planning ways to respond to an only child's career milestone. Anna had seen this call as a kind of ending, putting an end to a period of uncertainty. Now, among all the other things, she could look forward to a few days away. *Away. Really away. Fifty-five hundred kilometers east and a bit north. Home. Then back again, and ... space.*

In space, orbiting over the general part of the world where she was, an extremely expensive shoe box moved with the planet. It and the other members of its cadre were, in a physical sense, Anna's future.

===

Two: The Cliffs of Moher

Not many mornings later, Anna woke up in what had been her childhood bedroom. Outside the window, there was a view of Liscannor port and its boats. There were fewer of them than there had been, and they were almost all local fishing craft, now. There'd been more tourism while she was growing up, but with the general dispersal of people out into the countryside, towns that had been tourist places were increasingly occupied by those who wanted to be there permanently, working remotely for employers all over the world.

She got out of bed and walked to the window, and she looked first at the rough stone fence on the other side of the road. It wasn't very high, just enough to draw a line between traffic and not-traffic. Beyond it was the water and clouds and the land and houses across Liscannor Bay. It was very familiar. She stretched, turned to her open suitcase, and began to think about the day. *Today,* she thought. *Today, we go to Moher. And Lisdoonvarna for lunch.*

Her parents had been perfect. They'd greeted her as though this was just another trip home from college. Her father was as he always was: formal-sounding but affectionate. Now, he was adding just a bit of paternal pride to the mix. Her mother, Aoife, had turned on all her maternal charm, concealing, as she always did with family, the implacable, demanding, and successful wine importer that she was.

Today the questions that Anna knew were coming began to appear. The first day at home had been simply dodging around it, talking about family elsewhere in the world, culture, her father's emeritus retirement from the University, neighbors. But the elephant in the room was, of course, Anna's new ... job, career, life ... whatever it was going to be. Her mother opened the topic.

"So, dear. When do you start out?"

"Three weeks. It'll be be a kind of ... intake, I guess. Like orientation, at the start of school."

"Back in the Republic, I assume?" Her father knew the answer, of course.

"Yes. I'll be moving north, up to the training site. It's on a lake."

"One of the Great Lakes?"

"No, not this one. It's called Gogebic or something like that. Everybody just says *The Training Site*." Her old man made a mental note to look at a map, later, just to see where it was.

"Up there," Anna went on, "I'll get training on the ground, and in the last week, we'll actually go up. Up into orbit, I mean. Just orbit."

"We'll be able to look up and say *There goes our Daughter*, then?"

Anna managed to smile. "You can say it. But we won't be easy to see. Not from here."

"Where, then?" said her mother.

"We'll practice on some sites - you know, given places - in Arizona and New Mexico."

"Really? Why there?"

"Because there's not a lot going on. We're not looking for *people*, of course. We might see some, even out there, but we'll pretend not to. And then we'll practice picking places where we'd send equipment down."

===

Yet another meeting. At least it's virtual. General Gorsky looked down the agenda. The prep screen showed a list of topics related to policing the Starship project, across the globe. It said things like "Review pending legal actions," "Review new national participants (none current)," "Personnel-related actions."

The screen cleared and then displayed a physical meeting room, located in Brussels. This year's legal Commissioner was an ex-military officer, late of the Belgian army, and with a substantial background in jurisprudence. A few of the Legal Section team were physically present with her, the rest were, literally, all over the place. Gorsky was in her office, in the Republic's Security Branch headquarters, in what had been a major university town, now the Republic's national Capital.

"There is actually little to cover at this session," said the Commissioner. "There are no pending National applications, although there are suggestions that an African nation may be preparing to apply. In the legal actions list, there is a formal documentation levy against one of the Starship vendors. With our approval, it will be sent to the firm in question. And we have just received a complaint concerning an anonymous individual member of a Starship crew.

They talked over the document levy. It was similar to a subpoena, saying to one of the member nations, *find this document in your records and send it to us for review. And if you don't, we can fine you or throw you out of the club.* Since there was no longer another place to sell space tech, companies in that line of work were usually very interested in complying with the Program's requirements.

The group agreed that the levy should be sent, and that both they and the agreement-compliance people would review the response.

"Next, the complaint I mentioned. There is an anonymous allegation that an individual has, on at least one mission, brought consumable alcohol in his or her personal gear, and that the individual is sometimes observed to be intoxicated. The request is that we determine what actions the charter allows the Program to take, given the accuracy of the allegation" There were some blank looks, one or two concerned expressions. Gorsky spoke up.

"In the Army of the Republic, intoxication on Government duty is, obviously, prohibited, and when it's detected, the resulting action depends almost completely on what the potential harm is. To the individual and to the population. Do we know what level of responsibility the person holds?"

"We do not. We don't have a name, as yet."

"Then, speaking from my experience, we could consider a general reminder ... a re-statement, if you will ... of the policies regarding intoxication while on a mission. That sends a message that the activity is suspected, and it can, possibly, bring it to an end."

"Realistically?", another group member asked.

"Not very, I'm afraid. But it's a first ... hint. As long as we don't know who the person reporting believes is doing it, we can't take any direct steps."

"Other suggestions?" said the Commissioner. No one had any. "All right, I will ask the Program personnel staff to draft a message and provide it to us for review."

The meeting ended, and Gorsky signed off. She sat back in her chair and rubbed her eyes. Then she sent a simple message to another government employee. *He hasn't got enough to worry about*, she thought.

===

Elsewhere in the Capitol, what had been a university building had become Republic government space. An office in it was occupied by an older man, Otto O'Neill. He had a semi-circle of gray hair, leaving his forehead and the top of his head bare. He had no specific job title, and even though his body kept whispering "enough", he remained a critical kind of strategic and tactical glue, holding together the most important of the various government agencies, leading their people along paths that would have the most benign effect on the general safety and comfort. He and Gorsky had known each other and worked together for decades. What they had in common was a deep, mutual respect for the other's capability and intelligence - that and a shared goal to keep the Republic alive and in health.

===

It was a stark bit of landscape, the Cliffs of Moher. The tourist walk along the sea's edge took them along a path, *Burren Way*, then back to where they'd left the car. First, though, they stopped at a tower erected by a rich man in the nineteenth century. The view west, out toward the new world - where Anna had been for the last twelve years - showed a small island, and then just ocean. They stood looking for several minutes. Then the mother said "Shall we go to Lisdoonvarna now? For lunch?"

"Yes," Anna said. "Let's go." She looked back at the sea again. She'd always walked as close to these cliffs as she dared, looking down. The Atlantic washed against the rocks two hundred and some meters below. *Goodbye,* she thought, and they walked back to the car.

The drive north presented a mix of rolling farm land on the right side of the road and frequent views of the sea on the left. She was surprised how little the reversed traffic bothered her. *They still drive on the left,* she thought. *Otherwise, twenty-first century. Sort of.* She remembered her surprise, coming home from a year in the US, and finding that all the telephone poles were gone.

The road bent and twisted, staying close to the shore. There were no shoulders, for the most part, just drystone walls, small farms, what had been, her father said, a golf course. Farther on, they passed through a cluster of houses, the inevitable pub, and a monument to something. Always ahead was the same loaf-shaped scrap of white cloud. After a while, the road twisted inland, leaving the sea behind, and there began to be signs for Lisdoonvarna. *When I left here,* she thought, *I was still almost a youth. What would it have been like, staying?*

A bus, absurdly large for its setting, went past, headed for Moher. Then a turn north, over a creek, into town. Hotels, bars, houses. There was still a church, but the signs indicated it was housing a local museum. "So the church is shut down?" Anna asked.

"Well, they have exhibits there. The things people used to do. It's educational." Her mother sounded a little wary of the topic. The Father kept his mouth shut.

After lunch, they drove back to Liscannor, along a more wooded route. There were occasional views of mowed or grazed fields, with the ground rising to the west, stretching away evenly on the east. The sky began to turn gray. "Rain before we get home," her Mother suggested. *Of course*, Anna thought. *It's Ireland.*

They ran out of south road, and switched to a western, newer, faster one. *Tourist traffic built this. Where are they all now?* Ahead, the sky brightened, denying the Father's prediction. There was a little, very Irish town called Ennistymon. A bridge took them across the Inagh River. Out in the countryside again, it almost looked like an American Mid-western scene except for the traffic direction.

With one more small town behind them, they went north for a short distance, clearing the end of Liscannor Bay before turning back west once more. It was all ex-tourist here, with similar, whitewashed rental houses on the right and another golf course, of all things, on the left. Anna smiled at the sight of sheep grazing on it. A few kilometers farther they crossed a stream, and Liscannor began to appear. And then, suddenly, they were home.

The Father shut the car off, got out and stretched, said "Home is the sailor, home ... in time for tea." The Mother smiled. She'd heard that one many, many times before. Anna said nothing. She walked to the end of the drive and looked out at the bay. No rain clouds appeared. Just a scattering of those same white solids and stripes, decorating the blue sky and narrowing to some vanishing point, beyond the southern shore.

===

When their conversation ended, neither O'Neill nor Gorsky was especially wiser for it, but both had experienced a reminder of a general concern. One Starship crew member reporting that another one, unnamed, might have an alcohol problem was not a crisis, but it pointed to a question they'd both asked themselves when the Program kicked off: how would the internal workings be policed? Within the Republic, the generic answer to anything like that question was "The Security and Intel Branches get their heads together and fix it." But the Program wasn't just within the PR. Governments all over the planet had various stakes and responsibilities, and although the Republic was a major contributor, technically and even as a landlord for one Starship base, something like a substance issue on one ship was neither easy to address nor an existential threat.

But ... both of them knew of much bigger issues, things that, left uncorrected, could have much more serious outcomes.

"What's the count now," Gorsky had asked, "How many sovereign nations are we talking about?"

"Let me see," said Otto. "We have three in North America, thirty-one in the European Union, ten in the Asian group, plus New Zealand ... forty five, at last count. There are more in Europe, thinking about it, at least. It's not hard to imagine fifty voices, in a few years."

"There's a lot of people out there who used to be rich. And some who still are. We'd better keep our lists up to date."

"Yes."

"But ... this occurred to me the other night. Do you ever think of retiring? Of the effort to pass on what you do, hand it off to someone else?"

O'Neill looked at her for a moment. "And have no tasks, no to-dos, no meetings, just the day to putter around, planting something, pulling something out that hinders other things. Deciding to meet someone for a meal, or not to. Is that how it is?"

"I assume it is."

"I've never thought a great deal about it, that I remember. It's always seemed like a thing one did while waiting for ... some other thing." Gorski looked past him, toward one of his many bookshelves. On the second shelf, standing in the middle of several other works, was a hardbound volume titled *Wilfred Owen: The Collected Poems*.

===

The drive to Shannon Airport was not tremendously interesting. It was just miles of highway, southeast down toward the Limerick border, turning off just short of it. There was the inevitable *Now, do you have everything?* dialog, the *Let us know when you get there* requests. And finally, as Anna was going off to the gate, a tear or two in her Mother's eyes. For Anna, the change was quick and familiar, from at-home-with-the-folks-in-Ireland to the almost psychotic surreality where international airports live.

In the departure area, she sat, noting that there was at least a thirty minute wait before check in. She had things to read, of course, but as she settled in, her phone made its *incoming* noise, and it showed her a number in the Republic. *Oh, dear*, was her immediate reaction.

In fact, there was no cause for concern. It was the Program, and all they wanted was to confirm her travel north in three days, plus offering a few reminders of what she'd need to bring, what would be supplied. Essentially, it was a briefing on how she was going to get to the launch site.

"Bring a change of street clothes - wear them when you come in, no need to pack more than that. All your work clothing will be issued to you when you arrive at the site. You'll be flying out of here -" *Right, the Capitol field, not National Air Port, Anna thought.* "The Project has its own planes. Our driver will pick you up - confirm your address for me ... good, that's close to where the other person is. They'll call you first, then stop by for you a few minutes later. Any questions? All right, you're all set. Welcome aboard."

Anna's reaction varied between relief - things were underway - and an into-the-unknown sort of distress. The reality of it could be stated in a sentence: In three days, she'd be taken to an airport, she'd get on a PR government aircraft, and she'd fly 600 kilometers northwest, up into a backwoods part of the Peninsular Republic. *Three days*, she thought. *I'm packed up, at least.*

This set of internal quality assurance checks went on for a while. *What about ... Oh, right, I did that ... but what about ...?* Her flight was called, she got on the plane, it took off, turned west, and in a surprisingly short time, Anna was out over the ocean. *I wonder how long it'll be until I see an ocean again? From this close?*

===

He owned a large house on a large piece of land, looking downward and out over forests and hills. The state of Virginia tapered to its western end not far to the south, and a drive to places like Richmond or Washington was not a short one. Behind the house, there was a helicopter pad, and that used to be a solution to the distance problem. Today, there was nothing sitting on it. J. Robins MacIntyre forced that thought away. He'd managed to sell it, and he'd fired its pilots and maintenance people. Four of his financial advisors were unemployed as well, and the remaining one was only still around because there were questions about how much more of his money he could transfer to foreign banks.

A squirrel dropped something onto the deck, a foot from where MacIntyre was standing. He turned, saw what the disturbance had been, and kicked the acorn away. *Damn tree rats!* He looked at his watch. *Better get inside*, he thought. He was expecting a call or two. Even though the nearest road was half a mile away and the nearest house at least that much more, he preferred not to do business outside.

===

Three: Going North

And in three days, it began. When Anna walked into the passenger room at PR Capital, there was a sense of having crossed a line. Just in the last few days, she'd crossed several. She'd flown out of Ireland and simultaneously out of the European Union, crossed into Canada, and then flown from there into the Peninsular Republic. Now, for a while, at least, she wouldn't have to manage any more of that herself. The Project was about to pick her up, fly her up north, teach her how to do what she needed to do, and send her into space. All she had to do was show up.

Here in the Republic's Capitol airport, only one other person had shown up, riding out here with her. She was about Anna's height, plus a centimeter or two, slim, and with extremely dark hair, worn short in a kind of cap. Compared to Anna, she was darker-skinned, and with a face that suggested South Asian genetics.

"Hello," Anna said. "Are you going up North, too?"

"Yes, I am." The accent was as North-American-flavored as Anna's had become. "I'm Siriom. Barnes. My first name has something to do with infinity. My mother's a Sikh. And Barnes is just Barnes."

"I'm Anna Grover. I grew up in Ireland, but I've been over here long enough that I have to remind myself that I wasn't born here."

"I'm from the US, but ..." She waved a hand around. "... maybe I'd like to stay here."

"I'm going to use this work ..." Anna waved at the airfield. " ... to qualify for residency, here. My parents are Irish socialists, and they're okay with my being one officially" She paused. "I'm lucky they didn't call me Mary."

"Mary? Not for the obvious reason, I assume?"

"No, It would have been after Mary Harris Jones. But my mother was a realist as well as a Socialist. "Mary" is out of favor as a name, now. Like naming a boy "Peter or "Paul." So I'm just Anna. Anna

Grover."

Before Siriom could ask about Mary Harris Jones, a man in the PR's green army uniform opened a door. "Training personnel ...?" Both women nodded. "Out this door, please. Make sure you have everything you brought with you." As they went out, they could see a small general-purpose-like aircraft, painted green, and with the Republic's blue "PR" emblem on the tail. There was a set of movable steps in place, leading up and into it.

"Somewhat no-frills," Anna said.

===

MacIntyre's call hadn't gone very well. Two of the attorneys he used to employ were no longer available. A third one had managed to stay away from the planetary exploitation business - far enough away at least to avoid going to jail. But he wasn't the cream of the crop. "Listen to me, Lonny," MacIntyre said. "You're not listening. I don't want this damn thing to last, and I need good legal advice on staying out of trouble while I and some other people stop it."

"Yes, I do understand that. But the advice I have for you is this. You can't do what you want to do by filing law suits. It was hard enough before the ... trouble ... and the door is really closed, now."

MacIntyre glared at the screen. "I got a judge disbarred for making bad calls. There's a man who used to run banks. He's out of a job now because he got in my way." He didn't mention his ex son-in-law. That person had been in jail for spouse abuse when the pandemic hit. He and a hundred and thirty-four other inmates died of the infection. MacIntyre had gotten him into that situation, partly by law and partly otherwise. "Now, what we need to get done here is to decide if you're going to be part of this or not."

"That, sir, would be *not*. I'm sorry, but I try not to take baseless issues. And there's a matter of a hundred and twenty thousand dollars in fees that we're still owed. From the last ... business." He was being a little coy; it wasn't a case of "we" anymore. He was the only partner left, and the rent on the office would eat that up in short order.

His client's voice became extremely formal. "All right then. Send an invoice. I will seek counsel elsewhere." The call ended.

===

On the way up, the two young women exchanged more of their backgrounds. Anna's was more complex, Siriom's was slightly less pleasant. Anna had discovered, during her first year in the Republic's Department of Education, that if she did well, she could sum her graduate work with seventy-five percent of her schooling time in Ireland, then add on time from a teaching assistant position and credit for finishing her Master's degree ... and, if she wanted to, qualify for Residency.

"Residency?" Siriom asked.

"Almost citizenship. Everything but voting and serving in the Council. The elected body. As if I'd have time for that."

"So, you're ... basically here? For good?"

"I am. It makes my parents jealous. I get to live in a real socialist state. As opposed to all the pretend ones."

"Good. Good for you. I ... haven't met many people from here."

"Well, the borders used to be pretty absolute. But it's opened up more now, with the EurAsiaNA. The NA part means that the Republic has more points of contact with the US. Diplomatic contacts, even."

"It didn't, before?"

"No. Everything had to go through Canada. But now, it's easier to travel. And study."

Siriom glanced out the window. "What a bridge!"

"Oh, are we that far, yet? Great. That's the Mackinac Bridge. We're ... um, two thirds there. I think."

The conversation declined into mutual thought. Anna considered how fortunate she'd been, stumbling, in effect, into this society.

23

Today, her planning horizon only went as far as their destination, but at least she had a Peninsular Republic passport and almost certainly some kind of science career. If she wanted it. What about this other, pleasant young woman, though? Did she have that kind of ... comfort... to look forward to?

Siriom, on the other hand, was wondering about Anna. She hadn't mentioned any kind of relationships. Was that accurate, or was it a thing you just didn't bring up, here? She knew a bit about the Republic, about its nearly non-violent separation from the US, about its rigorously egalitarian society, about its gradual opening of ties with Europe and an even more gradual touching of fingertips with the US. This was a chance, she concluded, to learn more. *We'll be on the same ship, the same missions ...* She glanced at Anna. *Yes, I want to know this person.*

===

MacIntyre was not a happy man. He had been happy, several times in his life. They were the times when, from his standpoint, he seemed to be smarter than the typical human. In fact, he had some characteristics that were useful, abilities that could, in moderation, contribute to the general well-being. He'd backed large companies who employed a reasonable number of people. For most of his youth and middle age, there were still a large number of others who would look at him with a mix of respect and envy.

But now, the ranks of those who saw obsessive self-interest as a good thing - a thing to admire - were shrinking. The count of disasters caused by that point of view was simply too large to be missed. A lot of people were dead because of a few people like MacIntyre, and many of the MacIntyre-types were in jail. His psyche wouldn't allow him to admit it, but he was becoming part of an endangered species. And if he had known, he wouldn't have guessed that part of the danger was that he was Individual S339 on a list in the Intelligence Branch headquarters of the Peninsular Republic, and he was likewise known to the United States' Federal Bureau of Investigation.

===

"There's nothing down there but woods." Siriom was sitting across the center aisle from Anna, looking out the window. It had been three and a half hours, but now the plane was banking left, tilting the right wing up, clearly preparing to land.

"It's out this side," said Anna. "Kind of small, though." What she was seeing was a single runway, a series of rectangular buildings, and an unmistakable launch site: a large, round concrete pad, empty, and ringed with more buildings. There was no shuttle craft in sight. Beyond the buildings, there was a long, blue lake, running north-south for twenty kilometers or so. "Home away from home."

The plane finished its turn. The co-pilot looked back from the flight deck and said "Prepare for landing!" in a more severe tone than a commercial pilot would have used. *Right*, Anna thought, *A lot of the agency is military of one flavor or other. Here in the PR, anyway.*

With the plane on the ground, they were encouraged to check for forgotten gear and to be careful going down the steps. At the bottom of the steps was a civilian who greeted them and led the pair to a military-looking vehicle. "I'm Mike Strang," he said. "Formally, Science Personnel Intake Coordinator. I'm in charge of trainin' up here, this side of the Atlantic. We'll get you set up with your rooms, and then I'll give you the opening sermon."

The rooms were, not surprisingly, small, but they were rooms, not just bunks. Strang waited while they put their bags away, then led them on a quick tour.

"This building, by the way, is Residential One. It's all academics, all civilians. The next one down ..." he waved his hand ... "that way, is Two. The military folks live there. Across the road is Admin and the dining room. And the teaching spaces are at the north end." He waved the other hand. And of course, there's the shuttle pad and the in-and-out building. You get into the shuttle and out of it, goin' through there.

"We'll go over to Admin, now, and get your gear, bring it back to your rooms, and then we'll go back again to Admin for your actual, official, no kidding first briefing. Okay?" Neither of the women could think of anything to say except "Yes."

Their "gear" consisted of one large package each, presumably containing bedding of some kind, and a smaller bag of what Strang referred to as "personals." That turned out to mean clothing, all very civilian and quite light weight, plus some toiletries. "Still summer up here," Strang said, "No need for coats, yet, unless the weather goes nuts."

"This is ... uniforms, right?" Anna asked, referring to the bundles. "Should we change?"

"Nah. When you're on the ground here, you can wear what works for you. Put 'em on when you run out of clean gear of your own. You wear 'em on the Orbiter and the Star Ships, of course. They don't shed fiber, and we don't like fiber in zero G. Gets into things."

Twenty minutes later, they were back in the Admin building, sitting at a conference table. There was a large display screen, showing just the phrase "Initial Brief." What followed was a slightly modified copy of the Starship Program Curriculum Update that Kristin Horstel had presented to the Education Department people. Picking up from the "No Contact" discussion, it went on to cover the visit-a-star, observe-planets-if-any, send-robotics-down-to-likely-ones mission description.

The video ended. "So," Strang said, "That's the background. The *reality* is this." The screen showed a series of stills. One was a rectangular solid, seen from a distance, against a black sky. There was a row of something - circular shapes of a different color - along the top of the long axis, a couple of oblong ones at a lower level, and a row of larger circles along the bottom. It was tilted toward the camera just enough to show a large rectangular door on the short side. There was a reddish planet visible behind it.

"That's a starship. You're seein' it from the side, about a kilometer away. That top row is a big array of sensors, all sorts of 'em. The things below 'em are a couple of general imaging lenses. And the row of doors below ... that's where we launch things. Down to the surface. If there's a reason to. The big door on the end is the loading portal. All the gear and supplies and crew get on or get off from there." He paused for breath.

"We send science people - that's you - out in one o' these ships, and we fling it all off to a solar system where we *think* there might be some life-capable planets. Emphasis on *think*." The screen image changed, showing three engineering drawings of devices. "And these are what we send down to planets, if there are any. If we think there's anything to look at."

"The one on the left, that's your basic, no-crew orbiter. It gets in low, does nice 3D images of anything from the whole half-surface of the planet, right on down to about a square kilometer. If the sky's clear. Otherwise, it can only get good resolution in four or five square-kilometer chunks, dependin' on what kind of gas is in the clouds. So, that's our first look."

The screen changed to a lab table. On it, there was a device about a meter square, with a mix of dish antennae and lens openings. "Now, this is the atmospheric probe. It can get down to the surface, but it doesn't like to land. Can't get back up and move around, again. So it just hovers, takes images, records sound, samples the air - if there is any - and sends the info back up. It can move, too. Goes pretty damn fast. Sixty or seventy KPH over the ground, dependin' on the air."

"And we'll be running these?" Anna asked.

"Yep. You'll get to control fliers. And even better, you get two or three of these guys to run." This time the image was of a somewhat smaller box, equipped with a complicated-looking set of underpinnings, wheels, lens windows, and eight arms, two on each of the sides. "That's a rover, and it's your feet on the ground. It can image stuff, grab stuff, analyze stuff. It comes down on its own ... it's not carried by anything, but once it's on land, it can't go back up and fly off somewhere else by itself. All it can do is drive around. So one of the big things you'll do is decide where you want to put one."

"And we don't leave the equipment there, on the planet, right? When we're finished?"

"Mostly, no. The ship has a special version of the Orbiters. They come down, grab the gear, and pull 'em back up. Then they turn 'em loose in orbit. Not leavin' any evidence behind, you could say. Questions?"

"Not yet," said Siriom. Anna looked at the screen and said, "Where does the crew live?"

"Oh, yeah. Forgot. That whole top slice, where all the sensors are?" He flipped back to the first image. "All that level is mostly crew space. There's some science space up there, some engineering and comms people. Bit of Admin. And there's vertical shafts up and down among the levels. Okay?" Anna nodded.

"Then, that" Strang said, "is that. Now, let's go have a look at the real, on the ground, Dining Room."

===

It was an early morning, several days later. Anna was up and dressed, wearing her ship-board clothes, since both she and Siriom would be having another forty-five minutes or so with Mike Strang. Then they'd go up in an Orbital Shuttle to the training ship, the EO *Myra Tanner*. It was, Strang had said, somewhat smaller than the starships, but mostly because it didn't have their out-of-the-solar-system gear - just simulators.

"So the military people - ship's crew, you might say - pretend to take the ship off to another solar system, and then the science people - your bosses and you - take over and pretend to do science." Strang's phone buzzed. He didn't bother looking at it. "Shuttle's landin'," he said. "Any more questions? No? Okay, grab your gear, and let's get over to the pad."

The pad was, of course, the circular shape Anna saw as they flew in. Now, it held a rectangular solid with a smaller extension on one end of the long dimension. A shuttle was designed to land, unlike starships which were certainly not. The shuttle had six regularly-spaced, flexible legs with circular feet. At the moment, they were supporting the rest of the vessel.

There was an obvious set of steps and a door. Staff - mostly military - were doing things around the shuttle, and there were people, also uniformed, bringing things out from storage sheds. "That's your ride," Strang said. At the beginning of a paved path toward the shuttle, there was a sign: *Hinc itur ad astra*. Siriom glanced at it, looked again, and then laughed.

"What?" Anna asked.

"It says *From here the way leads to the stars*. In Latin. Sort of."

"I'll take your word for it."

There was a cursory check of IDs and gear, and then Anna and Siriom were waved out toward the pad. Crew helped them get up the steps and choose places to be. "Seats" wasn't an accurate term. Each passenger took a position along one side or another, using belts and clips to secure themselves and their gear. With gear stowed and both of them belted down, the two women waited for the launch. Siriom had asked Strang if he'd be coming along. He'd said no, he'd be down here, waiting to welcome another trainee. "He's getting his intake with us, even though he'll serve back in Europe. They're workin' out a problem with their shuttle, so he's breakin' in over here."

Outside, the sun was up and there was enough breeze to raise some minor wave action on the lake. "Kind of limited service," Anna said. She leaned back, then forward again, quickly. Out the small window - really a port hole - the scene was changing. The view of the lake extended across to its far shore. The shuttle was underway, rising straight up. "That was subtle."

"Really," said Siriom. "Somehow, I always pick the wrong side for sightseeing." She raised her hand. There was a decreasing sense of weight, less and less sense of muscles holding up the arm. "No refreshments cart, either, I'll bet."

===

In Liscannor, Anna's mother glanced at her watch. "Well, Anna will be up by now."

"Up?" said her husband. "Do you mean out of bed or off the planet?"

"One or the other." Her phone rang. "Excuse me, I have to talk to this ... individual." She accepted the call. "Yes, Guilio?" The father could hear an Italian accent, speaking rapidly.

"Yes, I know," Aoife Grover said. "And I think I pointed out very clearly the delivery requirements." There was a pause. Then she said "Listen carefully, Guilio. Non mi interessa. Capire? We have a contract. Get those twelve cases on a plane to me immediatamente. Nessuna scusa. Arrivederce." She closed the call.

"Italian isn't one of my languages," her husband said, "but I assume you were expressing your displeasure?"

"Oh, he's a silly boy. He needs a mother's gentle correction, now and then."

===

Nope, MacIntyre thought. He scrolled past a message from his ex-attorney. It was a request for payment, straightforward and to the point. *Suck it up, son. Not happening.* There were a few more notes from other people, most of them also irrelevant, and then one he'd been waiting for. He read it, replied "*Good. Let's talk,*" and - a rare thing, lately - smiled.

===

The shuttle approached the pseudo-Starship slowly. A screen showed the passengers a forward view. They were moving toward the end of a long rectangular solid. The ship's name was printed at the "top" of what was probably a door. It said *EOO Myra Tanner.* "Earth Orbit Only," Anna said. "That's reassuring. I'm not sure I'm Exosystem qualified, yet."

As the two women watched, the loading portal opened, the door moving "upward" into some sort of housing. The open area showed an empty, lighted space, looking very much like a garage. They had heard, prior to getting on the shuttle, a description of the arrival. They knew, for one thing, that they were to do nothing, stay in their positions, and wait for instructions. There was a completely unnecessary reminder that they were weightless, and that everything else was, also. Oh, and there was no air outside, and there would be none inside the portal until the door closed and it was replenished from the ship. *So stay seated.*

Got it, Anna thought. *Happy to oblige.*

It took a relatively short time to secure the shuttle to the floor of the cargo bay. The doors slid back into place. Panels on the walls, one each side, began displaying lights and symbols, one of which was the word "AIR". It was red, initially, and every few seconds, it flickered. After a few minutes, it suddenly turned green. "Cargo port secured." said a voice. "Remain in position." A few seconds later, the shuttle's forward door opened, and two people pulled themselves in. One of them had a device in one hand; she glanced at it. "Barnes?," she said.

Siriom said "Yes?"

"I'll assist you in getting out and up to level one. Grover?" Anna nodded.

"Tom will assist you. Both of you unlatch your restraints. Tom, you go first."

===

It didn't take that long, really. All Anna had to do was allow herself to be taken by the hand and gently pulled along toward the door, her assistant having done this multiple times before. Once out of the shuttle, she could see a door ahead, standing open. They approached it, and she was pulled through, into a kind of warehouse. "This is the general storage area," the young man said, "Level 3. and over there ... " He gestured left. "are the launch tubes for probes and rovers." *Over there* was a wall with a door in it. "The level tubes are in there." He pointed ahead.

"Level tubes?"

"Like elevators. Up or down. But they're not powered. They're just tubes. You pull yourself along with the grips. Pick the one on the right, or you'll bump into people comin' the other way." Anna could see that the things they were approaching were, in fact, labeled "Up" and "Down." There were doors leading off to right and left, too.

"What are those?"

"Simulated Location shifters. Like engines. That's how we'd move the ship if we actually did move it." They'd reached the level tubes. "How do you feel?"

"If I don't turn my head quickly, I'm ... okay, I think."

"So you go first, then. I'll help you get in the tube, and then you just use the handles to pull yourself up. You're gonna go right past level two, then get out on one."

"And I'll know it's level one ...?"

"It'll say that. On the wall of the tube. And there won't be any more tube. And I'll be coming up behind you."

"Oh." In fact, it was relatively easy. She looked down once and saw her guide and behind him, Siriom and presumably her assistant behind her.

At the top of the tubes, a woman met them. She wore the same not-military clothing as they did, and her name tag said *Greene*. Anna looked at her closely. It was a familiar name, and so was the face.

"Welcome aboard," she said. "I'm Marjorie Greene. I'm the Science Lead for the training unit. Let's get you set up with your rooms, and then we can dig in a little farther." She looked at their tags, *Grover, red hair; Barnes, black*, she thought. The people who'd been helping just turned and went back down the other tube.

===

First level was a compromise. The majority of the space was taken up by four long rows of one-person rooms. At one end, there were combinations of washing and toilet spaces, and there were also a pair of "offices," places where the business of the community could be conducted. There were grab-handles everywhere, circles of cable that you used to propel yourself. "We'll go straight down this center hall." Greene said. She watched their efforts to comply. Barnes was doing all right, Grover seemed to be having a bit more trouble. She hadn't pulled hard enough on the first grip, and was just coasting slowly toward the next one. She got there, though.

"Give yourself a little more velocity. It takes some practice, and there really isn't any way to get it except on-the-job-training like this." Anna nodded. With an adjustment or two, the three of them grouped together at the entrance to a hall. It was completely lined with doors, and the nearer two of them were standing open.

"So, Barnes, the first room ..." She pointed at it. "... is yours. "Grover, you're in the next one. See if you can pull yourselves into them, and I'll just help if you need it. All right?" They nodded.

Anna said "Excuse me, Doctor ... were you teaching at the Capitol campus?"

"Yes, I was. Two-plus years ago."

"I was in a class you taught. Exobiology."

"I thought your face was familiar. Good to have you aboard."

The training began with procedural things. Eating times, sleeping times, exercise, meeting the rest of the crew, and, of course, actually doing research work. For both Anna and Siriom, that meant first learning how to evaluate remote data - images and readings collected by the ship's sensors - and those in orbital drones, sent into low positions over a planet. Working with the atmospheric probes and surface rovers would be step two.

Doctor Greene helped Anna into an analysis "desk", and showed her how to strap down. "You have to walk a fine line between not hindering your use of the controls and not floating away," she explained.

With that explained, she moved on to the task itself. "So, you log in here - that way, the launch people know who's asking for what, when you get around to asking." Doctor Greene gestured around the control space. "You've got your orbiter on-line ... your satellite" She pointed at a trio of screens, arranged in a one-high, two-below setup. "The top one is whatever you ask the orbiter to look at. Go ahead and turn that one on." Anna touched the obvious "on" button.

"This is one I like to start with." Greene leaned in and touched a "Recents" control. The targeting screen showed a rectangle of reddish brown surface area ... somewhere. "Now, that looks as though it might be interesting, even though it's obviously pretty dry." It was, in fact, very dry-looking, but near the center of the image, there appeared to be some water. "Let's take a look at that puddle ... " She zoomed in.

It did seem to be water - spaces of the screen showed a bluish-gray, very irregular shape. "The last person I showed this to thought it was art of some kind. But it's real. If you saw something like that on a planet, how would you evaluate it?"

"Well," Anna said, "The first thing I'd want to know is whether that gray / blue / white imagery really is open water. So, I'd use reflectivity tests, bounce some HE laser off the surfaces, see what the algorithm thinks." This was all echoes of her earth-bound education.

"Good."

"And then ... there's a lot of lateral lines, up here." She pointed, and Greene zoomed in. "There's blue, gray, some dark blue or black features. And north-west to south-east stream beds. If there isn't water now, there was, not very long ago. Can I move this around?"

"Sure. Just slide your finger tip."

"Now, that ... " Anna pointed. "... that looks like a lake, with part of the bed exposed. So, a half-filled lake. And down here ..." Another move. "That's got to be live water ... flowing out of this triangular place and down a stream bed. But it just peters out ... in desert."

"Very good. So, would you send a probe down there? Or surface gear?"

"Maybe. I think I'd look around a little more, see what else might be going on, first."

"Right. In this case, if you zoom out a bit ... that wheel, there ... you'll see an indication of cultural activity." Anna rotated the control, the image expanded, and green letters appeared: *Karlamilyi National Park.* "What?"

"Western Australia. This is a seasonal lake ... very seasonal. The first European to report it called it Lake Disappointment. The native people - the Martu - call it Kumpupintil. There are water birds, reptiles. And it's endorheic ... it doesn't connect with other bodies of water. When there's rain, then there's water. Otherwise, not."

"I guess ... I wouldn't start here, then. I'd want to see if there were places with year-round water. Or what looked like it, anyway. But I'd make sure I recorded this location. Something to come back to if ... if there just wasn't any water anywhere else."

"Yes, that would be my initial call, too. It's a fascinating set of images to look at, but I'd want to have more promising places examined before I spent any surface assets on it. Now, let me just call up another ..." She touched a panel. " ... See what you think of this. I'll have you work with the image."

The surface screen showed a rectangle of a planet surface. "You can make it a square if that's useful. And assume you've chosen this as an insertion target, already. Where you want to send a probe and a rover." The orbiter screen showed another broken, rough landscape. On the right, a low range of hills ran down toward the center, showing tangled, branching lines and no obvious indication of plant or other life. The rest of the image was apparently level ground, but either cut down or bulging up - not easy to tell - with serrated features. They ran in clusters, primarily left-to-right.

"On a real mission, you'd have been looking at all of that for a while, at this level, and at higher magnification ... hit that "Zoom" button there, once." Anna did. A portion of the image appeared, showing the surface features more clearly. *"That's not likely to be wind action,* you'd have said to yourself. *That looks like water erosion to me."*

"It does," Anna said. "All those little cuts and branches. The flatter areas ... that might be some wind, there ..." she pointed at the screen.

"Could be. Right. And you can make an arrow move around on the image ... put your finger on the "Track" pad there ..." Anna pressed it with her right index digit. A green pointer appeared on the screen. "Now just move your hand around ..." She did, and the arrow followed where her finger pointed. "And you can touch that other pad ... over there ... and it'll mark where you were pointing."

"Okay, I point at things. What does that do?"

"It gets elaborate. Simplest thing is, it marks that spot for you. And you can zoom in ... push your stick forward, there." The image expanded. "So, that's as far as you can zoom in from orbit, without changing the orbit itself - coming down toward the planet. And you need authorization to do that. Looks kind of like a face, doesn't it?" She pointed at the center of the screen.

"I don't see ... oh, is that the eye? And an eyebrow?"

"Yes. That whole high spot there is about three K long, north to south. Looks like, I don't know, a kind of post-impressionist face in profile. The long jaw line there, and the eye. And all those little valleys. They look like hair."

"And, just a guess, I don't report seeing anything like that."

"Not formally, no. See anything else, though, that might be interesting?"

"Ah ... lots of little cuts ... small ridges ... maybe water, at some point."

"Look at all the edges of the image, too. Don't get locked into the center."

"Okay. I'm seeing ... oh! Yes. I see a *road*. Probably."

"Yes. Down in the lower left, there's a couple of dirt two-tracks. Department of the Interior people run around out here, from time to time. But if you zoom out again, it all goes away. Gets lost in the pixels."

"And so I have a limited number of probes and rovers ... and I have to decide where to insert them. Would I send a probe to look at those roads?"

"On your first couple of planets, you'll get input on that. People who've been doing it for a while will look at the big picture ... zoom out all the way ... that slider, there." The image began slowly expanding, away from the surface. "There, that's Santa Fe." A gray stripe stretched across a very dry-looking valley. It was sprinkled with white dots - houses - and there was an obvious road running diagonally across the screen. "So that's a definite CAI, there. *Cultural Activity Indicator.*"

"It certainly is."

"But on the basis of those little straight lines we saw, you'd get someone else's opinion, probably send a probe first, then a rover. See what's really going one. Those are certainly interesting features. But if you see something like we have here..." she pointed at Santa Fe "... well, you'd want to jump right on it, I guess. Everybody on the ship is going to have something to say about it."

"Yeah," Anna said. "I can imagine. It's a jade idol, for sure."

===

"Good morning. Is the General on the phone?"

"No, Captain, go on in." General Gorsky's desk Sargent liked most of Intelligence Branch crew and this one in particular. *Always ... in control* was the impression.

Cordell opened the door enough to look in. "General," she said, "Can I have a minute?"

"Sure. What's up?" Gorsky had been hoping, in fact, to hear some news.

"Well, Sir, we have a plain English conversation between the primary S339 individual and another person, using a name that shows up in

EU court records."

"In the EU. Interesting."

"Yes, we think the primary has exhausted his US ... support. He's reaching out. And the general sense of the conversation is assessing EU Starship personnel for involvement. In negative actions."

"And is he still doing this in clear?"

"On this message, yes. He does have encryption, but we're beginning to think he may sometimes just forget to turn it on.

"Idiot."

"We hope so, yes."

===

"All right," said Doctor Greene, "let's try a few images that are less ambiguous, life-wise." Anna and Siriom were acting together, this time. "Team analysis has worked out pretty well, to the point that we're teaching it, now. So, the game here is that you'll act jointly on what someone else considers possible surface life." She brought up a long shot across a set of sharp cliffs, falling vertically down to a large body of water.

"Imagine we've seen this area as orbital images, and somebody - me, for example - thinks there might be some kind of plant growth on those rocks - the high ones, well above the water. So you've been tasked with putting probes down to look at them - no point in rovers, yet. No use trying to land on those extreme surfaces." The cliffs appeared to have a dip angle of thirty-five or forty degrees.

"Hanging on by their finger tips. If they have any," Siriom said.

"So, go ahead and move in with the probes. You've each got one. And, by the way, this is simulated. It's a real place, on earth, but you're moving around in a virtual space. It's not something below us, here."

The next ten minutes were at least fun. The closer the probes got to the rocks, the more obvious it was that something other than rock was there. "That's got to be chlorophyll," Anna said. "Algae? Or actual plants?"

Siriom nodded. "Looks like it. And it's only on the highest parts of the cliffs. Maybe least likely to get washed off by wave action?"

"It's a clear boundary, anyway." Anna said. "Look at that sharp point, there, for example. It's got nothing on it. But the surfaces above it do have green ... oh, wait ... the low one sticks out and ... maybe shields the ones above? So the green stuff up there doesn't get drowned?"

"And higher up, there's a ridge or an edge, anyway. And the greenery on the back side ... away from the water ... is healthier looking."

This went on for a while, with both of them bringing simulated probes zooming in closely, showing that whatever the green was, it had something you could call "leaves" or "flat surfaces" or "sun collectors". And the more the rocks were vulnerable to wave action, the less of it there was. "Without getting a rover-like-thing in there," Anna said, "I don't think we can be sure, but it looks lifelike to me." She turned to Siriom. "You think?"

"I do. Life, probably."

"Good," Greene said. It is, in fact. Hardy little plants, growing on cliffs at Dunquin. Your part of the world, Anna. Great Blasket Island is about four kilometers southeast. But that was a warm up. Now let's try something a bit more ambiguous." The views changed.

"Oh, my," Anna said. "That's ... uninviting."

"It is. Again, you've got probes, but assume that this time, you can drop rovers, too. You have to fly your probes in first, and then pick points for the wheeled gear to land."

The visible surface was all grays and some reddish-brown points, and it was fragmented into layers and pieces. There wasn't a straight line in any of it. In the center, there was an obvious shaft, roughly triangular, and running down into the surface and out of sight. Right outside it, there was a smaller rounded area, higher than the general surface plane, and exhibiting the most color.

"So, what do you think? See if that flat ... sort of flat ... area southwest of the mound will take a rover? The top of the mound doesn't look level enough." Siriom pointed her cursor at the image.

"Okay. And another one over here?" Anna indicated a flat place east of the mound, somewhat below a terrace of rock that might have a vague greenish tint, if you looked closely.

"Let's give it a shot."

A virtual rover, with Siriom driving, descended slowly to a point below the red hill. Anna sent hers over to the base of the second feature. Neither one yielded helpful information. The red hill was just that - red. If you could get to the top of it, you might find some kind of ferrous material, but iron oxide wasn't usually an indicator of life.

To the east, Anna got her rover down almost to a surface, then aborted. "Can't land. It slants too much downward. Let's see what the probe thinks."

"And while you're at it, maybe a pass across the mound? Try imaging tricks to see if that's really metallic?"

"Fine." That took another fifteen minutes or so. Nothing they saw offered any indication of life.

"Doctor Greene," Anna said, "What do you think about that ... hole, there? Would you approve a probe trying to fly down there a bit, if we requested it?"

"If this were real, probably not. They're disposable, but we like to keep them around while we're working on a site. Or at least wait until we've done everything else we want to, within their across-surface travel range. But you get a point for asking."

"So this isn't real?"

"Yes and no. Is there anything else you'd look at? Before calling it non-life-supporting?"

"I don't ... think so. Siriom? Do you see anything?"

"If we had days to fly around, there might be ... microbial indications. But we can't just drive the rovers here and there ... it's so broken up. We'd have to pick them up with the Probes, fly them thirty or forty meters to some other surface, and set 'em down again. How much time would we be spending with something like this, Doctor?"

"Probably a day or two. Especially if the planet surface is *all* like this. And it might be."

"So my call would be, forget the rovers. We look hard at as much as we can, using probes, then move on to another location. Anna?"

"Agreed. I've seen less interesting surfaces, but not all that many."

"All right," said Greene. Again, if this were real, you'd have a valid case. Reasonably fast aerial analysis, leaving surface investigation out unless it's warranted. Your supervisors might disagree, but that's another story." She paused. "Do you want to see the real thing?"

"Sure."

The view pulled back and out very rapidly. It showed a tree. "That's an extreme closeup of a sycamore tree, growing in a back yard. About a minute after I took that, we identified life." A similar zoomed-in image appeared, with a large ant crawling out of the central hole.

"Life! Evidence of life!" said Anna.

===

The training went on, taking the bulk of the working "day" ... seven hours with a one-hour break for lunch, etc. ... plus "evening" discussions after a meal with all hands. By the end of their fifteen days, both Anna and Siriom were doing well, not only at spotting life or its absence but also at just the reality of a zero-gravity existence. On the morning of their last day, they got physical examinations, checking on weight loss or gain, muscle mass, respiratory function ... all the issues that lack of gravity and excess of human contact could create. As the shuttle was docking, Greene showed them their successful-completion records, congratulated them, and said that she was coming down, too. "Turns out, I'm going on your mission. I came up here to stand in for a trainer, and he's coming back, so I get to go life-hunting with you."

"Great," said Siriom. "We'll see you on the dark side of the moon."

"Yes. And there'll be room upon the hill." Greene pulled herself off to finish more training reports.

"I'll be damned," said Anna. "What are the odds that three people, floating around in orbit, would be tagging a twentieth-century progressive rock band?"

"Behold a dream, the dream is gone."

===

Another meeting. The pay's the same. Gorsky looked at the screen. "The security responsibilities for the Starship program are now being seen as less well coordinated than they might be." The speaker was the same ex-military person who always chaired these things. "They would like to see changes, preferably structural. This need was made clear by the program management Council. The idea of a unified, newly created security organization was turned down on grounds of expense and, frankly, feasibility." Gorsky maintained a neutral expression.

"So, I would like this group to propose an alternative. I know informally that what the Council would like to see is a split along east and west lines, with the Bolten and the new ship being under the responsibility of a North American legal organization, and Orwell and Booth having a similar group based in Brussels. General Gorsky, do you have a reaction to that?"

Oh, I do, indeed, she thought. "The Republic has a security agreement with the other North American members. Under its terms, we provide security on a physical level - securing the base, transport to and from it, background investigations, the basic things that the council mandated. But the EU and Asian members wanted more local control. We agreed to that, partly because we would have had difficulties with stationing our people outside the Republic, and also that we understood the other parties' desire for local efforts. What I suggest is that the EU and Asian members explore a similar model, with an emphasis on cross-communication and cooperation at high and medium levels." *A captain in the PR picks up the phone and calls her opposite number in Beijing.*

"This would also satisfy my government," said the Chinese member. "Our people have some experience in working with the Peninsular Republic. And it has been productive." *Right*, thought Gorsky. *We knocked down a people-trafficking thing together.*

There was more discussion. The Europeans were handicapped by the sheer number of governments that would have to play together. The Asians had a smaller group, and they were all inclined to follow China's lead, since China was footing most of the bill.

"So what I believe we are saying is that we propose two ... or three? ... security organizations. North America and Europe plus Asia? Or Europe and Asia as separate groups?"

"Our position is that a separate North American group is essential. We can easily work with another one or two groups, as the Council approves." Gorsky was getting good at this diplomatic saying-things-without-saying-them business. In fact, the western partners would rather have just two security groups, but since they knew that the Council wanted that, too, then let the Council say so itself. The others generally nodded, said similar things, and expressed a consensus.

"Very well. I will present that idea to Council, and I will report their reaction, in writing, to all of you. Are there other topics to discuss?"

There weren't other topics. Gorsky closed the call, then made two of her own. The first was to her contact in the Republic's External Relations group, essentially, their State Department. She provided them with the conclusion that had been reached, and she asked to have it transmitted to a specific US Senator, through formal channels. Then she switched to a more rigorously secure mode of communication and called that same Senator.

He picked up the call. "Well, General, nice to hear from you. How are things in your world?"

"Interesting, as always, Senator. Just wanted to let you know that the group accepted our formula, and they'll be pitching it to the Council at their next gathering."

"Very good. I'll be sure to support it. Thanks. And how's your partner? The empress of education?"

"She's fine, digging deeply into the collective psyche of our youth."

"Have to get her down here. Ours could use some digging. Enjoy the rest of your day."

"And you. Goodbye."

===

Four: Of Moose and Women

Back on the ground. Things definitely felt heavier. Siriom and Anna walked, slowly, from the shuttle pad to a point near the launch site's central road. "I can feel some of my legs again," Anna said. "But, um ... there are these benches, all along here. I didn't notice them, going up. Maybe we could sit a minute."

"Yes," Siriom said. "We should."

They sat down. After a minute or so, just staring straight ahead at pine trees, Anna remarked that she really didn't know what she was going to do with her time off. "Two weeks, right?"

"Two weeks. And I haven't got anything in mind, either. A question: where *are* we, anyhow?"

"You mean, in the base? Or in the universe?"

"Well. We're in the ... Republic, right? In the woods. By a lake. True?" She was still breathing rather heavily.

Anna nodded. "Right." (a deep breath in) "In the woods. Seriously in the woods."

"There's a town. I saw. On a map. Berg... something." Siriom pointed generally north. "Fifteen K. That way."

Anna exhaled, then breathed in again. "I could probably walk fifteen meters. Maybe. Not fifteen K." They sat there for a few more silent minutes. Then a voice said, "Well look who's back." It was Mike Strang.

"Hello," Anna said.

"So ... you got plans for your time off? Need anything?"

"We could use (cough) a clue, I think." Siriom looked at Him. "What do ... people ... do here? After being up?"

"Mostly, after about twenty-four hours doin' next to nothin', they sign out a vehicle, and they go have a few nights in the big city."

45

"Big city?" Anna said. "What big city?"

"That's right. I forgot you weren't a native of these parts. I mean that jewel o' the Eighth Division, Marquette. This time of year, it's an easy, snow-free hundred and eighty some K over that way." He waved a hand off to the East. "Couple of hours drive and you're there."

Siriom smiled. "That sounds ... good. Hotels?"

"Why, sure. Restaurants, bars. Three or four of 'em, at least. And all the Lake Superior you care to look at. Presque Isle, Presque Isle Park. Go a bit farther north, you can get out onto a point and look at Little Presque Isle itself."

Anna took a deep breath. "Do you ... mind if I ask ... are you from around here?"

"Me?. Hell, no. I'm a Detroit man. But if I'm gonna look after the trainees, I have to know the amenities, right? Drop in on me tomorrow, when you're feelin' more adventurous, and I'll get you a staff car."

===

"So ... a hundred and eighty kilometers of this?" The view out the vehicle window was a long gray strip of pavement, stretching to the horizon, mowed strips alongside, and ... trees. Lots of trees. Anna was driving, having volunteered to start out. They were on their way, headed east and a little south, on what seemed to be an interminable two lane highway. "Is this someplace?" Anna asked.

"It's, um, either Topaz or Ewen, depending on which sign you believe." Siriom was navigating, following their progress on the dashboard map display.

"Ah." Some time passed. "And here? It's a crossroads."

"Well, it's a place ... Matchwood. It says. Not a lot here, I'm afraid. But brace yourself. Coming up is ... Ewen."

When they got to Ewen, it turned out to be a four corners with two of the largest motor vehicle dealerships Anna had ever seen, regardless of the nationality involved. There was a body shop and a building supply, and then more blacktop and trees. Eventually, the terrain became slightly less flat, and they crossed a small river. Later, they passed a place whose entire economic basis seemed to be a post office and a bar.

On and on they went, following PR highway 28 until it became PR highways 28 *and* 41, continuing on past a more modern-looking polity, with businesses dating from only a few decades before. Past that, they saw a small sign: "Big Friendly Rock." And there was, in fact, a big rock. Someone had painted "BFR" on it. They elected not to stop.

Finally, they reached what could be called a suburb of Marquette, and they stopped to charge the vehicle. It was getting on toward lunch time, but Marquette beckoned them onward. The city was one of the last large polities in the PR to retain its old urban sprawl. There was, to put it crudely, too much land and too few people. Auto service businesses could take up as much real estate as a small neighborhood in the southern cities.

"Is it all like this?" Siriom asked.

"Don't ask me, I'm just a lass from the auld country. I think we have to get down to the lakefront ... in fact, let's get off this damn highway." She turned to the left, onto a numbered street.

"What was this? Seventh?"

"Yes," said Anna with an assurance she didn't really feel.

"Then, go right ... right here. On ... Baraga? ... Street."

"There's a church over there." Anna said.

"I thought you didn't have them here?"

"*Not as such*. That's a quote from something. Anyway, they didn't demolish the buildings. The PR just took them over. That's probably a school, now. Or a clinic." Anna knew things like that because of her education, once she'd signed on in the Republic. They weren't quite as jolting to her as they might be to others, since the only thing her parents disliked more than fascism was, in her father's words, the "bloody church."

Siriom didn't appear to care about metaphysics, either. She was looking at street signs. "Ah. I see ... wait! I see water up there! Ahead." In fact, two to three blocks ahead of them, the blue and white sky came all the way down and drew a visible horizon with Lake Superior.

===

MacIntyre was, for his time, an old-fashioned criminal. Compared to world averages, he was also a long-lived one. Bumping up against eighty years, he'd made a career of doing the most obscure but still profitable crimes he could arrange, getting others to do the actual work and dropping them like rocks afterwards, whether they got away with it or not. He wasn't anything like as rich as the really big villains, but he'd never been charged with - let alone convicted of - anything. His approach was to provide the funds, define the schemes, take a cut, and hide it. And he abstained from fads; he'd never owned so much as fifty cents worth of any crypto currency, and his nest egg was partly in rock-hard funds and bank accounts. The rest he kept as a buffer. In a safe, like the ones people use for firearms, there were six million and some dollars worth of hard currency. It was in US dollars, Euros, and Swiss francs, mostly.

Earlier this morning, he'd handed off an envelope with some of the Euros in it. It was sealed, and the person who received it went immediately home, took a cab to Washington Dulles, and got on a plane for Brussels.

===

The hotel was close in, along Marquette's Front Street. It was a rectangular solid, made of a medium-brown brick, and with a sense of age, not in a derelict sense, but literally: a building that had been there for a while. The desk was glad to see them, had their vehicle taken around to storage, and directed them upstairs. They'd opted for individual rooms, mostly out of a sudden enthusiasm for privacy.

"Doctor Greene mentioned it," Siriom said. "That we'd want some personal space, the first few days. Something bigger than the broom closets on the ships." Anna just nodded.

It had gotten a bit past lunch time, and so they did a minimal amount of unpacking, then met back at the desk. "Where's a good place, close by?" Anna asked the clerk. "Within walking distance." The suggestion was a pub two blocks south and one east, down to the waterfront, good view of the lake. The desk clerk was used to people from the base coming here on leave; he knew that guests might want to walk somewhere, but not far.

They walked the proscribed distance down Front street, then turned off toward the lake. The ground went down rather quickly, with the bay opening up as they went. In fact, the whole left side of Washington street was a series of eating places, and the recommended one was right at the bottom. There was a waterfront park immediately outside, and beyond that, obviously, the lake. As they went into the pub, Siriom asked "So, is this kind of a tourist town?"

"I ... don't really know," Anna said. "I've never been north of the straits before, let alone out here."

"The straits?"

"Straits of Mackinac. Where the Upper and Lower peninsulas come closest to each other. We flew over it, when we came up here."

"Oh, right. The big bridge. Seven kilometers, or something."

"I guess. I'm just a poor girl from Clare. You're at least a North American."

===

After they'd eaten, they spent more time walking around the city, going south to Newhouse Park. For different reasons, neither of them knew that it used to be "Father Marquette" park. With the passage of time, the Republic was beginning to have a roster of its own deceased leaders after which to name things, and Seventeenth

Century Jesuit Missionaries weren't on the list. The current name honored a long-time head of the Army of the Republic.

They ate ordinary but acceptable lunches. As they walked back toward the hotel, Siriom suggested a detour up Main Street, scouting for dinner spots. The first block was unpromising, being about fifty percent parking lots. There was an older building, identified as a "depot" but apparently full of medical offices. "I guess this used to be some kind of train station," Siriom said. They walked on, and then discovered that "Main Street" didn't mean what it might have at some earlier point. For one thing, it ended abruptly at a cross street, and for another, there was very little commerce on it.

"Huh," said Anna. "Not very ... *main* ... really."

"No, although ... there's a farmer's market over there. That's sort of hip, I guess."

They turned right,walking back toward the harbor, and immediately began to pass restaurants, bars, and retail stores. The next cross street was even more retail and food oriented, using older but nicely maintained one or two story buildings. From there, they climbed the slope on Front Street, back to the hotel. The other streets heading west away from the lake seemed to be as unexciting as Main.

"Funny place," Siriom said. "I wonder what it's like in winter?"

===

At the launch site, Doctor Greene stuck her head into Mike Strang's office. "So, Grover and Barnes went on leave together?"

"That's right. I pointed 'em at Marquette."

"Fine. They'll be working together, might as well relax together, too."

"Well, yeah. But I recommend that little outin' for all the new folks. It's the only place to go, really."

===

Next morning, the "new folks" had breakfast together, then asked the desk clerk about out-in-the-country drives, or lake-shore views, or must-sees in general. It was a woman this time. "Okay," she said. "You have a vehicle, right? You could drive up to Big Bay. The views are nice. And there's a historic marker."

"Like, colonial history?" Of the two, Siriom had more experience with explanatory historic signage. US parks were covered with it.

"No. Or, well, there might have been something like that, there, but this was a bunch of local boys, fighting with the Army. They lost. The locals did."

"Which army? The US or the PR?"

"Oh, the PR. The locals got bad information. They thought they'd get help from some of the people who'd left. Livin' over in Canada. So they tried to take over the Security post up there. But it was a lie. People got killed, and people in the Government got arrested. It wasn't good."

"That's interesting," said Siriom. "I'm new here ..." She looked at Anna. "Did you know about that?"

"A bit. I didn't know it was close by."

"Well, it's forty kilometers. Kind of close. It's a two lane road. Paved, I mean," said the Clerk.

"Maybe next time?" Siriom said. She turned to Anna. "Or would you like to try it?"

"Wars and battles aren't really my area. How about if we just go and look at the lake? Like the gentleman suggested yesterday."

===

When you set out to reinvent a country or a state or a neighborhood, for that matter, one of the things you have to deal with is authority. Historically, many groups in the process of creating or managing a new political system equated authority with violence and the combination of the two with freedom. Revolutions or invasions of all kinds, from the protohistoric far east and middle east to the Twenty-

First Century, have involved armed groups imposing things on other groups.

Whether the original developers of the Peninsular Republic's constitution were consciously emulating earlier thinkers or making it all up as they went along, they did play with the idea of power coming out of the barrel of a gun. However, the power they used to separate from the US had nothing to do with guns, *per se*. The lever was a technical capability, used to force the US into cooperation. Armed civilians had nothing to do with it.

Instead, the new constitution included a general prohibition on personal weaponry. It provided absolute bans on possession of any "projectile propelling weapon or other equipment" by any individual except serving, on-duty members of the Army of the Republic. It had one immediate effect and several long-term ones.

First, people who felt they couldn't live with it took the offered government assistance and went south to the US. Anyone, in fact, who disagreed with the Separation for any reason could pack up and go, taking their movable possessions, and receiving compensation for any real estate they owned. Early on, it removed a substantial part of the cranky population, and it left the government in possession of a large amount of land.

In the longer term, it fostered a kind of psychological evolution. The people who remained were those who didn't want to own weaponry, and that meant that their offspring were brought up in that environment. The schools taught the idea that an armed public was far more dangerous than a republic whose constitution was locked in place, one where you were born with a set of rights, and those rights were yours, period, for life. In the Republic, laws could come and go, but they had to take direction from the Constitution, and the Constitution was intentionally developed to be *once and for all*. Nowhere in it was there any provision for amendment.

===

Gorsky reached for her coffee. The mug was where it usually was, just where a hand would find it without needing visual guidance.

Sadly, there was nothing in it. *Oh, well. I need to get up and walk a meter or two.* She locked her desk machine and got up. Outside the office, she exchanged a smile with her Admin and headed for the coffee stand. As she was pouring, a young woman with a Captain's badge arrived. "It's that time of day, Sir," she said. "caffeination."

"It is, Meg, it is. How's S339?"

"Slow, General. There are ... resource problems. Filling positions, if you see what I mean."

"Any actors identified yet?"

"Not since ... since we talked about it."

The whole floor of the building was a closed area. So many Intelligence Branch people held clearances and so much of the work was classified that the so-called open areas were actually smaller and one floor down. Even so, the two women didn't go any further into the topic. S339 was now a critical investigation. It had funding by the Starship project, it was secret at a high level, and J. Robyns MacIntyre was its central concern.

===

Over dinner, Anna and Siriom talked about their day, the fishing boats along the coast, the lighthouse on its peninsula of black rock. They'd taken some pictures, although as they'd note later, none of Anna's included Siriom, and vice versa. There were shots of blue water and small waves; there was one of a dead whitefish, dropped on the beach by some unidentified bird of prey. Siriom had a picture of a shingle-sided house, backed right up onto the lake. Anna had views from a park: three rocky islands, two hundred and some meters offshore. Looking at them, Siriom said "No life on those planets. Probably. Unless you count seagulls." Anna agreed.

They did a bit more driving, looking, driving some more. They stopped to eat the sandwiches they'd brought. Eventually, they turned around and went back. It had gotten to be dinner time, somehow.

They picked a place in town, had a bit of wine, ate things that were wholesome, if not epic. When they left the restaurant, it was getting dark. Street lights were on, and the city seemed somewhat more lively. It was four blocks back to the hotel, and they walked slowly, saving their legs for the last, rather uphill, distance. "You know," Anna said, "That wasn't very tiring. So fifteen days in zero G equals ... two and a half? ... of recovery?"

Siriom smiled. "Let's hope so, anyway. See you in the morning. Breakfast, and then whatever hundred kilometers it is, back to the base and our fellow space cadets."

===

It was the same hundred and eighty-some kilometers, past the same rural fields and forests they'd experienced before. Siriom drove this time, and the conversation was mostly of the mission. It would be mission one for both of them, and each one felt, at the same time, some anxiety and a determination not to show it.

They went past a small place called The Cozy Inn, then the trees closed in again and there was nothing else - no other vehicles, no structures, nothing. Anna was about to say something about that when Siriom said "Hey! What?" Ahead there were flashing lights - the red-blue sequence that meant "Security Branch working." Anna suggested slowing down, quickly, and approaching with caution. As they closed in, they could see three or four emergency vehicles, SB personnel, and some kind of towing truck. And there was another, bigger vehicle, skewed partly out of the west bound lane. In the middle of the road there was one young woman in uniform, holding a "STOP" sign.

They stopped. The trooper walked up to the window, glancing down at the car's identification and its "PR GOVT" signs on the door. "Good morning," she said. "There might be a bit of a delay, I'm afraid." She paused just a beat, checking to see what kind of officials were inside. *No uniforms*, she thought. *Official business of some kind, but probably not emergency duty.*

Anna leaned over, wanting to be part of the conversation with this authority figure. Her colleague had, after all, just a bit more than a month in the country. "What happened?"

"A moose decided to butt heads with a truck. We're still cleaning up." She pointed back at the situation. We've got one lane open, but there's a couple of vehicles waiting to come through this way. Once they get by, we'll pass you through."

"Wow. Is anyone hurt?" Siriom asked. "Besides the moose?"

"The moose did not survive the incident. And the truck driver has a bloody nose, probably a pair of black eyes, too. Hit the steering wheel. But the truck is driveable, once we get the victim's body out of the road and the vehicle hauled back onto the pavement. It's got both front wheels down in the ditch, right now." As she said that, first one and then another civilian truck came up past the crash, moving slowly. "Any minute, now," the trooper said.

"Does this happen ... a lot?" Siriom asked.

"Not with moose, so much, no. But in the spring ... the deer are all over the place. We get one or two calls a day, then, all over Eighth." She brought her phone up to her mouth. "Understood. One vehicle coming through west." To Siriom, she said "Okay, folks. You're clear. Just drive slowly through there. And watch out for the wildlife."

They went cautiously by the crash and on their way. The Corporal in charge of the incident called his trooper. "Any more on your end?"

"Negative, Sir."

"That was a Government car. What were they?"

"Uh, sorry, Sir. I don't know. They weren't Army, anyway. No uniforms. Might be the Starbase thing, over by Bergland. I warned 'em about wildlife."

"All right, Griffith. Keep your eyes open over there."

"That was kind of sad," Siriom said. "I mean, for a big animal to just ... have to be ... hauled away."

Anna nodded. "Agreed. We're dangerous neighbors. There should be signs. *Beware of the Humans.*"

"MacIntyre." He answered his calls with just that name. No one who might call him would be familiar enough to use his first name. *Or know it, even*, he thought. The caller wanted to send him a message and to remind him to read it and delete it. He said "Yeah, yeah" and hung up.

The message itself, once he ran it through a crypto filter backwards, was deliberately obscure. *One possibility detektad Man on crew drinks. Could be actor one. Looking for other.*

He was only slightly encouraged. For one thing, his person in the EU either had no spell checker or the code and decode software was buggy. But either way, it meant that there was some progress. MacIntyre knew that the first thing you needed was someone inside the target organization with a social problem. Drinking would do.

===

Five: Out of the System

At the base, the time went by. Every day, there were discussions, lectures by experts in this and that, more familiarization with the research gear, and several emergency situation briefings. Siriom named the latter events *what to do if you see a moose* drills. Initially, only Anna knew the reference, but in a close group like the StarShip crews, memes spread quickly. By the time Doctor Greene used it in a report, "moose drill" had become general parlance, meaning "a bad thing."

One of the events for Siriom was a discussion with Mike Strang on the subject of futures. "So, you're here ... I mean here in the PR ... on a research thing. We call it a *Temporary*. That means that as long as the research goes on, you might just as well be a Resident. Anybody explain what that means? Here in the PR, I mean?"

"It was ... said, I remember, but I'm not really sure I understood it."

"So, as far as people who live here ... I mean, live permanently. As permanently as humans live anywhere, that is ... as far as that goes ... there are four categories, and most people only care about three of 'em. One is *Juvenile*. You don't care about that, because you're over twenty-two years old. One is *Resident*. Means somebody who's got full rights to everything, except votin' and bein' elected to Council. One is *Citizen*, meaning a person with Resident status *and* a fourth-level degree - that's like a Bachelors' in the US - and who did national service - more about that in a minute - and, well, who *wants* to be. A Citizen, I mean. Not everybody wants to. But if you're a Citizen, you can vote in our elections, an' you can even run for a seat in Council, if you want to. He paused for breath.

"Now, you're - at the moment - here on status number four, *Temporary*. That means that you're a Resident, in effect, with all that goes with it, but only under whatever conditions were in the agreement you signed, including how long you're still workin' on the project."

"Okay. I remember that part."

"Good. I'm bringin' this up because you're goin' out on your first real mission. And I know you people don't get a lot of time off, up there, to think about things, other than the science. But besides all of that ponderin' you have to do, think about this. If you do good stuff, whatever that means for your job, you'll have the opportunity to apply for Resident. It's not a guarantee you'll get it. And for all I know, you might not want it. But keep it in mind. And as part of that keep-in-mind process, use your time off between missions. Use it to look around the PR. See if this is a place you might want to stay. And that's all I've got to say on that."

"Thank you. I will. Look around, I mean. Right now ... all I really know, all I've had time to learn about the PR ..." She made a circular movement with her hand "... is that you should watch out for moose."

"Always a good idea," Strang agreed.

===

The trip up to the real starship was the same procedure as it had been, going to the *Myra Tanner*: Get on, sit down, strap in. The difference was that instead of being the only passengers, Anna and Siriom were just two of nineteen. The others were either existing crew returning to the *Virginia Bolten*, or people coming in from other ground assignments, or they were other first-timers. Doctor Greene was among the old hands. She boarded and settled in across the aisle from her recent trainees. "I said I'd see you on the shuttle, didn't I?"

Anna nodded. "You did. It's reassuring." Siriom nodded, too.

"All of this will be just like going up to the *Tanner*. More of us, of course. Crew level and Science level are one and two, three is cargo, launch, the location shift units ... all the same. It's just a bit bigger, though. Since it stays on mission longer. We have to store more food, more launch units."

"Do we get on ... embark, I mean ... in any kind of order?" Siriom asked.

"The shuttle crew deals with that. They'll call the third level people off first, then us. So that we don't get in each other's way, in with cargo and all. Supplies came up yesterday, of course."

There was the usual reminder to secure themselves - "This craft and personnel will shortly be weightless." - and, shortly after that, they were. *A* full *mission*, Anna thought. *Three weeks weren't really all that ... bad. I can cope with more.* She would, of course, have to. Nothing but a serious illness or accident would get personnel back to Earth ahead of mission's end. *I asked for this,* she reminded herself.

===

It could have been any conference room in any organizational building anywhere in the world. It was an interior space, windowless, and capable of being locked. In fact, it was in the European Starship base headquarters, eight and a half kilometers southeast of Brussels, built on what had been a horse racing track. The *Renbaan van Groenendaal* breathed its last in 2001, after bettors found it easier to lose money on-line. This nineteenth century Royal property wasn't really set up for mass events, anyway. Other things had been tried, but only the Starship Council had the money and the need for headquarters space and a launch facility. Just as the North American location was referred to as Starbase Elizabeth Gurley Flynn, this one was called Raumhaufen Clara Zetkin.

At the moment, the conference room wasn't locked; the meeting was about nothing classified, sensitive, or even particularly interesting. It was about an update for the starship "engines," the Location Shift Units. Each vessel had two identical units, a primary and a spare. They were capable of quite precise shifts in a ship's position, in galactic terms, but for fine changes - moving slightly, with reference to a single planet, for example - they weren't as fine-grained as they could be. Consequently, the update was intended to improve that local maneuverability.

Like any professional software development group, the project management included representation from the client, the developers, quality assurance, and management. There were two people from the military Starship flight crews, three software engineers, one software tester, and a pair of program directors, one from the Europe/Asia group and one from the North American team. The meeting's topic was simply the process for implementing the upgrade when it was ready.

"So," said the European project head, "the deployment will require that personnel from Development be present at a Starbase where a ship is to be upgraded. They must go up ... " He gestured towards the ceiling. "... with physical media containing the new software, installation code, and security confirmation. Once there - on the ship- it takes twenty minutes to install the change and confirm it. Then, *boom*, you're done. Correct?"

"*Boom* isn't exactly how I'd describe it, but otherwise, yes. That's the procedure. QA?"

"Yes, that's right," the test engineer said. "We'll have people on the ground who can confirm the install remotely. I'll bring up this one point again, though. It would be good if we did more than just confirm that it's there."

===

On board the EV - Exogalactic Vehicle, starship, that is - *Virginia Bolten*, people got settled into their personal rooms and located their work areas. Gear came up out of cargo. Systems were turned on and tested. Anna and Siriom had device-control stations - meaning *desks with screens, buttons, etc* - on opposite sides of the second level. People stopped to introduce themselves to a new face or greet an old one. "Like the first day of a semester," Siriom said.

"Yes, but all one big class."

The two newest of the new people were among those anchoring themselves along the sides of level 1, preparing to hear the leadership - Doctor Greene and Ship's Captain Anthony DiBiasé - brief them on the current mission. Greene was dressed as she always was onboard: dark gray tights and a similar shirt. DiBiasé wore much the same thing, except that the clothing was black and he had a small, billed cap.

"Welcome," the Captain said. "This is the sixth mission for the Bolten, and this time, my friends, I hope we can not only find something, but that it's visible with the naked eye." There were smiles and a couple of chuckles. In the five previous missions, the ship had visited seventeen potentially life-supporting exoplanets, and it had recorded exactly one with what appeared to be single-celled animals, swimming around and eating what appeared to be single-celled plants. DiBiasé made an over-to-you gesture at Doctor Greene.

"I share that objective, Tony, and it's a pleasure to be back aboard. My time on the training ship wasn't wasted. I got to pick lovely places on Earth to use as examples of barren, lifeless deserts, and I did manage to coerce two new ecosystem analysts to join us. Grover, Barnes, wave a hand or something ... "

"Welcome to both of you," the Captain said. "We're not quite a full Marian legion, yet, but we'll get there. And we *are* shipping out with a full crew, this time." This got a few more smiles. On the previous mission, the science lead who was going to step in while Greene was away had been injured in a vehicle accident while he was on his way to the launch site. There wasn't time to replace him, and two of the senior research people had to step in.

"So ... " Greene said. "The big question we always have at these gatherings is, *Where are we going?* This trip, the answer is *out here.*" There were display screens everywhere on board, and one of the larger ones lit up.

"There's the Orion Arm, where we live, and out here ..." She had a pointer. " ... is where we're going." A shape like a scythe showed up. "We're going inward a bit, into the Scutum-Centaurus arm." There was a small reaction from the team; some had heard this already, others hadn't. "We're not going far along it, but there are these five star systems that look promising." Five bright spots appeared. "All of them are G-type, main-sequence stars, and the group that makes these target choices is *fairly* - their word - confident that there are planets."

"So," said DiBiasé, "let's go snoop around." Again, there was a murmur, but this time a generally positive one. Anna was fairly sure she heard someone mention jade idols, and perhaps someone else whisper "moose."

===

MacIntyre received another message, this one distinctly offline; it was in a sealed paper envelope, showing a canceled EU stamp. There was a card inside, with the front having a generic *Thank You* message. Inside, there was a handwritten note: "Danke, Onkel James! Ich schicke Bilder vom neuen Haus, wenn sie fertig sind." All MacIntyre cared about was that initial word -"*Thanks*" - and the Dusseldorf postmark; he didn't bother to translate any of the rest of it. *So you're on board, eh? Good.*

He shredded the card and its envelope. Then he brought up the desktop machine he'd been taught to use by a colleague, typed a reply - *You're welcome. Keep me posted.* - and then ran it through an encryption application. He had no real idea what that was; a colleague had given it to him when they were doing business, assuring him that it made things unreadable by those who shouldn't read it. He pointed it at an email address and hit *send*.

===

Early "morning". Clearly, the word didn't mean a lot on board the *Bolten*, but there needed to be terms for the chunks of a twenty-four hour period. Anna strapped herself loosely onto a workstation and stared into the retinal scan. It blinked a green light, loaded her data and preferences, and began to boot up. "All right," she said, aloud. "Let's do a little sightseeing."

The planet below was the second of two in this initial star system, auto-named *NeoFrisia*. The first planet, *NeoFrisia01*, had been farther out in its orbit, and it was, to be blunt, a frozen hell. It was essentially a ball of rock, with some areas of powdered rock ... what you might think of as sand ... just for variety. At first glance, there was no water, no foliage, not much ground relief. You might have said to yourself, *That's one ugly bowling ball.* And as the analyses began, that impression held up. Twelve days of scanning, measuring, hypothesizing, and general pondering convinced Greene and DiBiasé that the taxpayers funding EurAsiaNA would get more for their money elsewhere. They'd given the star its name, *NeoFrisia*, selected from a random list of human place names. Now, the *Bolten* was in orbit around the planet they were calling *NeoFrisia02*. And it looked somewhat better.

A large screen showed an image that Anna had picked from the seven hundred and twenty eight that Doctor Greene had given her. At its northern edge - applying the human standard of *up is north, down is south* - there was a large rock outcrop. The feature was a two-point-twenty-one kilometer strip of what the geology people thought was sedimentary rock, running East-West, and with a high peak of about seventy kilometers near the center. By itself, it wasn't especially interesting, but at its feet, there were strips of anomalous green. Similar things were showing up all around a belt at the planet's center, making a green stripe about eighteen hundred kilometers wide. The orbital gear couldn't be conclusive, but it sure as hell looked like foliage.

This was perhaps not an earth-shaking discovery, but it was the first suggestion of life that the voyage had provided. The first planet had been dead, dead, dead, as far as could be determined. But this might be the one! Anna thought. *It's got green, and it's the first we've seen.*

She'd been watching results from one particular orbiter for something like nine hours, with a three-hour rest-and-think-about-it break. She'd had something quick to eat and, with her mind made up, written a surface examination plan, gotten it approved by Doctor Greene, and was now ready to push the button, metaphorically speaking. In fact, the launch room had to push the buttons. She selected Third-level Launch-room on the communication control.

"Yeah, Anna, Launch Chamber!" The two military people who actually fired things off toward some helpless planet had a lot of sitting around to do. Until one of the research folks said shoot, they just kept the devices - orbiters, probes, rovers - loaded in tubes and ready. So Anna's call to them in their third-floor launch room was a welcome bit of action.

"I'm programming a probe in tube six and a rover in zero, right ... "
She clicked on a surface mission plan screen. "... now. Requesting
launch from six and zero."

"Wait one ... " said the launch person. Two individual screen icons
blinked green on Anna's display. "Launched."

"Thanks. Time for more coffee. I'll check on the hardware again in
thirty."

"Understood." The launch lead closed and locked the ports. "Finally
decided to shoot. Reload six and zero, P and R, standby status".

"Right, probe and rover, six and zero." The number two launch
person was less enthusiastic. *Float around, shoot 'em, reload. Get
lunch. Story of my life.*

For Anna, at least, time in the lab was very much abstract; it might be
0140 hours or 1750 or 2300. Everything was lit the same way,
regardless. And even if there was a star nearby - in an astrophysical
sense of "nearby" - there weren't windows for its light to enter.
Working in orbit around a planet was a binary experience, alternating
between the elation of discovery and vast amounts of analysis. So
far, it had been all the latter and none of the former, at least for the
people looking for life forms. The geology people were more
enthusiastic, but even they hadn't found a reason to do any soil
sampling.

Siriom, was in the same situation. She and Anna had been alternating
time at the workstations, and, in between, time at the old screen-and-
keyboard. There was thesis work to do and the management of data.
At the moment, Anna's focus was on the planet below, circling
around its star, rotating just often enough to give any individual spot
on its surface a week-long day. The Virginia Bolten was there above
it, sitting in a nearly geosynchronous orbit, and "imaging the bejesus
out of it" as the imagery team put it.

The summary results of from-orbit investigation were, so far, not
encouraging: Atmosphere: Yes: oxygen; carbon dioxide and

monoxide plus traces of other gases: insufficient for human respiration. Bodies of surface water: none observed. Underground water: undetected. Observable life forms: possible areas of apparent plant life. Animal life: none observed. Cultural evidence: none observed.

Bluntly, it was a planet, slightly smaller than Earth, with air, sort of; no oceans, lakes, rivers, puddles - it was waterless, at least on the surface, and there was nothing to suggest, so far, that it had ever been much of anything else. No jade idols. Now, Anna was going to see whether a particularly obvious patch of green terrain might have something that could be called vegetation.

Thirty-six or so hours ago, airborne probes had begun sending back ground-level imagery, closer in and in better detail than the orbital stuff. The ground itself was as strikingly uninteresting from close up as it had been from orbit. It was dry, sandy, and mostly level right up until, here and there, the dirt abruptly vanished under three-meter high "grass." At least it looked like grass. It was quite tall, yes, and kind of yellow-green colored, and it resembled ... grass. This was more interesting than anything else observations had turned up, so Anna was instructed to send a probe and a rover on their one-way missions. *Check out that grass,* she thought.

===

Gorsky and O'Neill were having a chat in her office, for a change. Otto didn't tend to visit other parts of the government in person, but he enjoyed coming over to Intel Branch and seeing the calm, cooperative way the group dealt with each other.

Gorsky leaned back in her chair and said "Our friend, S339, thanked someone for something. And asked to be kept posted. That's all we've heard recently."

"He's being fairly terse."

"Yes. But I'd rather have him saying something, even it doesn't mean anything. He's one of those used-to-be-rich folks we were talking about. It's when people like that go all quiet that I start to worry."

"Agreed. Do we have any other little hints?"

"Well ... Meg Cordell thinks he's looking for vulnerabilities. Chances to make the Starship Council look bad. *Why* is only a guess, right now.

"The investment theory?"

"Right. It is like a drug, isn't it? "

Otto smiled. "From the first deal over a mess of pottage, this sort of thing has had its winners and losers."

"Right. Or as I heard someone say, years ago, as useful as a stainless steel pickup truck."

===

It took four hours, give or take, for the two devices to get to ground level. Anna did other things for a while, got something to eat, and then went back to her work station. She was able to watch from one of their satellites as the probe deployed its stabilizers and began horizontal flight, moving close to the surface, near the edge of a stand of "grass." She was looking specifically for tall things that might present danger to the probe. The rover hovered above, tracking the probe, waiting for Anna to approve a landing site for it.

She watched the monitors. They represented two half circle views from the rover, 180 degrees forward and 180 backward. A smaller screen showed the ground immediately below the machine, and another one looked straight up, staring into a featureless, pale blue sky. There was nothing interesting below the device or behind it, but ahead, a wall of foliage and bare rock stood out.

Anna began recording verbal notes. Another set of monitors provided controllable views from the probe, and that view moved around in an automatic pattern, two meters off the ground. Nothing below seemed to be hazardous. The grass was surrounding and partly obscuring some reddish-brown boulders. They showed closely-spaced lateral striations, aligned with the ground. *Something abraded things here,* Anna thought. Wind or water. "Hints of erosion on the observable rocks," she said, recording her real-time notes.

Not far behind the boulders and the grass, the ground rose sharply, up to the top of a ridge. Its face looked exactly like the rocks, brown with a red cast, and there was nothing at all but the slope's face. "The foliage doesn't extend up the ridge face."

A rover's undercarriage could handle fairly extreme terrain, but ... *Is the surface rock, or sand, or what?* Anna asked herself. She moved the rover away three meters, then pointed the probe's sensors at the ground. She reached up to the top of her console and pressed "Impact Assess."

The probe immediately ascended another five meters, then fired a projectile into the ground. A cloud of dust rose, then fell away. Anna brought the probe down, looking closely at the impact. There was a barely visible dent, with a small circle of debris thrown around. "Impact assessment of terrain indicates near-surface rock substrate," she said. She flew the probe around to the far side of the rock. More grass, giving way to more sand. "Apparently vehicle-safe. Moving rover in."

"Probe 14 moving ... see location data ... viewing thirty to one-sixty degrees north. Confirm that from-orbit-observed feature does resemble Terran jungle grass, growing out of the soil as many single stalks and ... growing upward several meters ... branching into three or four separate leaves or blades ... fanning out from the central stalk. Leaves ... zooming in ... leaves taper to a sharp point at the end. Analogy to large terrestrial grasses holds up, visually. Apparently rooted in at least top levels of soil. Landing rover."

The wheeled vehicle landed and began to approach the stand of grass. It seemed unlikely that it would be able to get in among the individual plants without doing physical damage to the stems, but it would be useful to peek in and see what the ground looked like. She grasped the rover's remote control - essentially a joy stick - and moved it forward, toward the grass. Something flew across the camera display. "What the hell was that?!" Something else struck the rover with enough force to register on its motion sensor. Then something else obscured the camera, momentarily. Without necessarily making a decision, Anna reversed away and hit a call button - essentially a "Doctor Greene to Monitor Five" request. As she was saying that, the exobotanists, both of whom had been watching her display, floated up, looking extremely interested.

===

Meg Cordell sat in her own workspace, watching a Starship program review. Gorsky was in her office, on screen; Meg was neither visible nor announced. The topic was *Delivery and Installation of Location shift Software Update*.

The presenter, the Europe/Asia group Program Director, was talking about objectives. "The specific work done here to upgrade the software has been limited strictly to location shift granularity. Although there are other proposals pending, this particular improvement has been carefully limited to its specific requirements." One of the research leaders looked a bit sour. She had a pair of life-likelihood sensor system upgrades that she'd tried to add on, but without success.

"This will allow us to conduct testing here, and to then perform installation for the Starship units as they become available for upgrade, here or in the North American facilities. Doctor Scott?" He made an over-to-you gesture to his NA colleague.

"Thank you. The requirements for this - which is the first software change we've rolled out to the Starships - include extensive pre-installation testing at the module level, then a round of full function tests on static Location Shift simulators, followed by a live test using the European group's Earth Orbit Only ship. Since the sole requirement is to narrow the distances over which a shift can be accomplished, the local ships are obviously ideal for proving the concept. The requirement is, after all, to allow much finer-grained movements within a star system, and that's what those ships do. In our star system, I mean." Everyone did, in fact, know what he meant.

The presentation went on for almost an hour. When it ended - with both directors affirming their approval of the deployment plan, Meg shut off the machine and went to see Gorsky.

"What did you think?" the General asked.

"Well, in and around all the language, the plan is to bench test the code, install and run it on Shifters in the training ships and move them around in orbit."

"And ...?"

"And then install it in the Orwell, the Bolten, and the Booth as they come back in. They're making the assumption that if it works in a ship that just does Location shifts around our sun, that's one hundred percent test coverage."

"As the old ironic question goes, what could go wrong?"

"I don't know, General. And neither will they."

===

It was getting crowded around Anna's station. Doctor Greene and others were there, either holding on to grips or strapped into positions at monitors. The rover sat where it was; nothing was going on around it, now, and it seemed unharmed. There had been another attempt at moving closer to the grass, and the same sort of thing happened: the grass appeared to attack. Above, the probe was hovering.

"Let's try that again," said Greene. The probe gave one view and the rover's cameras another as Anna repeated the approach. What they all saw, the people and the devices, was the grass appearing to defend itself. Within anything less than a meter, the rover was assaulted with the sharp leaves, the plants on the outside of the thicket lunging at it. When it drew away, the attack stopped.

"So, okay," the lead botanist said. "Somehow the stuff senses movement. At least on the ground. I don't think we want to see if it attacks the probe, do we?" There was general agreement that they didn't want to do that. "But what in the hell does it use that ... behavior, I guess ... against? What's around to threaten it?"

"Has to be something mobile," Greene said. "Something that ... eats grass."

The conversation went on. Suddenly, Anna said "Hey! Look at that!" The rover's camera was pointed at the same part of the grass that it had approached, and one of the blades of grass had broken. It was lying on the ground, about two meters away. Now, a small gray thing ... to human eyes, at least, some sort of animal ... was coming out of the thicket and moving forward. "Wow!"

There was excitement, consternation, private concern on the part of those who'd been reporting the absence of animal species ... this was certainly an animal by the strict definition, anyway. It had, as they could see, fur or something that looked like it. Its body tapered down from back to front ... assuming that the front pointed in the direction it was moving. It had four feet. It even had a pair of things that resembled eyes. It looked, to put it Terra-centrically, a lot like a rodent. It stopped when it reached the end of the broken grass blade. And then, it started eating it.

"Doctor," Anna said, "Can you pan the probe around? See if there's any more broken grass."

"What ... oh. Yes. I see." Greene had taken over the probe. She sent it in slow passes, well out of grass range, looking for downed stalks. There weren't any. "Somebody has to clean up the dead soldiers? Is that what we're seeing?"

Going out on a limb, Anna thought. "I might say ... symbiosis."

"Yeah." Greene paused, then turned to another science member. "Steve, will you go and see if Siriom is up? We ought to get her down here, too."

===

Siriom was up, technically, but was still pulling her shirt on. "Just a minute," she said. An hour ago, she'd been looking at what might have been stream beds, but they turned out to be wind erosion artifacts. She filed that conclusion with Doctor Greene, then went off for a nap. She thought it would be Anna at the door. "Oh, Doctor

Merrill. What's up?"

"Come and see what Anna's turned up," he said. "Doctor Greene wants you to jump in, too."

"Oh, great! What is it?"

"She's looking at some attack grass. And it has a little friend."

===

Another meeting. Gorsky was, by profession, meeting-angst-proof, but adding the legal aspects of the Starship program to her membership list had expanded the boundaries substantially. She was now in a meeting that had been scheduled in haste, with a request for legal and law enforcement personnel to attend.

"Greetings," said the person running the show. "My apologies for the short notice, but the Program has received a proposal that is of substantial interest, and they'd like the opinions of our members, particularly those with legal expertise, regarding it." It was the kind of sentence that stresses translation software. Given the number of native languages represented by the attendees, the resulting text could have been much worse.

"A group of physicists and Starship experts, based in France and in Italy, have proposed a sub-program, one whose goal is to - using their term - *scrub away* the remains of inessential objects in Earth orbit. It would call for, *one*, designing and building small, un-crewed versions of the Starships. *Two*, providing them with what the group refers to as grappling and controlling gear. *Three,* collecting as many now-illegal legacy commercial satellites and other orbiting craft as their gear can accommodate. And, *four*, shifting out of the solar system, leaving the captured objects in inter-stellar space, and coming back for more." He paused. No one said anything.

"They emphasize that this has reached the proposal phase, only. But they would like to hear opinions from the Program in general, and especially from, as I said, the legal and law enforcement experts."

If this had been an in-person meeting, this would have been the point at which people looked at each other, waiting to see who would speak up first. After a second or so, Gorsky took a deep breath and began. "That's certainly an interesting idea. One thing that occurs to me is that some of those orbiting devices are still functioning, presumably offering services that people still use. Does the group address that set of cases?"

"We asked that question, yes, and the group agreed that there would have to be a taxonomy concerning the specific objects to be targeted. A means of classification, mutually agreed."

Good luck, Gorsky thought. "Yes, I believe there would be such a requirement. And once it's created and agreed upon, within this group and within the Program and its member groups, and then ratified by their various governments, it might be useful to proceed with the concept, its review, the budgeting processes ... " She paused, making a circular motion with her right hand.

"Und so wieiter," said a German member of the group. "And so on," echoed the software.

=====

Back at the monitors, Greene and Anna were working out next steps. "For one thing, " Anna said, "I'd really like to know where the water's coming from. If there is any, I mean. The ... animal ... might be getting enough, just from the leaves. But they don't look very wet."

"No, they don't, "said Greene. "But it could still work, I suppose. We have mammals that can manage without much."

"Yes. An oryx, for one. But they still have to have *some*. Can I try running the rover around to the other side of this ... patch of grass? Just to see if there's anything over there. A puddle or a damp spot or something?"

"Sure. I've got Siriom coming to help out, anyway. You check the back, and I'll get her a rover of her own." Anna backed the vehicle away from the grass, then started driving it off to the left, looking alternately at its camera feed and then the probe's overhead images.

Greene called the launch room. As she was doing that, Siriom floated into the control lab.

"What's going on? Have you got an actual critter?"

"Oh, hi. Yes, it's a ... a rat, or something. About that size." She waved at the screen in front of her. "Not here, right now. I'm going around the back of the grass patch. But ... wait a minute." She stopped the rover, then sent the recorded video of the animal to another monitor. "Watch that while we get another rover down there. For you."

"For me?"

"Right. We're going to need all the eyes on this we can get."

===

This was only the second confirmed life of any kind, that year, for the Virginia Bolton, on any of the targeted planets. The other one, on a previous trip, had been a kind of microscopic eco-system, promising, but with a very long evolutionary road to travel. And here, they had not just one but two species, apparently co-dependent, and visible with the naked eye. Greene kept pulling different people in, hoping for answers to new questions. Since the area around the target patch of grass was virtually identical and all of it appeared dry as a bone, they asked the subsurface imaging people to see if they could identify any hope of underground springs. They didn't find any, but their work did show that the roots of the grass were extremely long, going far down into the ground, well past the point where the imaging could follow.

"I'll bet that's the deal," Siriom said. "There's water so far down there, we can't detect it but the grass can reach it. I mean, why would they expend the energy on those long roots if it didn't help?"

"Okay," said Greene, "but still ... we haven't been here long enough to talk about seasons. What if there's a rainy one? What if there's a downpour or two, things get soaked, and the grass can live on it through the hot, dry period?"

"No surface evidence of that," Steve Merrill said. "There'd be gullies, stream beds, lakes, erosion ...". Merrill was Greene's second in command.

Anna was hovering, holding onto a container of coffee. "I had an idea ... one of those how-you-gonna-test-that notions."

"And...?" said Greene.

"What if there is, actually, water in the ground. Way down. And the plants absorb it. And the rodents eat the dead plants and maybe, the young shoots, too - if there are any."

"And?""

"That's how the rodents get their water. They process it and then urinate it. On the ground. And the plants ...". She made a kind of accepting gesture, both arms forward, palms upward.

Doctor Greene blinked. "A locked cycle? They just keep ... handing it off? But what ... "

"And, like Siriom said, there could really be *some* water down below, just enough of a flow to keep the cycle refreshed. So it doesn't just become whatever kind of uric acid substitute they have here. It gets, like I said, refreshed."

They all looked at each other. "It's worth ... proposing," said Greene. She looked around. Nobody seemed to have a better idea. "How about this? You two ... " She gestured at Anna and Siriom. "... write it up as a hypothesis, or ... hell, make a joint thesis out of it."

"Sure," Merrill said. "with all kinds of caveats, *contact restrictions prevent conclusive biological analysis ... etc, etc. .., but we propose that ...* "

Anna frowned. "How would that work ... My major prof is at PR Department of Environment, Siriom's is ... where is it?"

"East Coast Combined University. The Boston campus."

"I'll pitch this to your schools." said Greene. "I've got contacts galore at our Department of Education, and one of them has channels to ECCU. " She looked at Siriom. "And if they ... won't play, we'll get

DoE to put a review group together. You wouldn't mind a doctorate from our shop, would you?"

"Oh, no. Not at ... not at all. That would be ... fine."

===

Six: Another Day, Another Planet

The work went on. NeoFrisia02 was carefully imaged and described. And along with the various flavors of scientists and sailors, each of the StarShip missions also included a writer. This was a person skilled in description from visual evidence and also in human narrative forms and customs. The task was to make the knowledge gained by the mission staff comprehensible to humans in general, not just to the academic and military worlds. On the *Virginia Bolton*, the person with that task was a man in his late forties, Ralph Lochram.

"Tell me about the conclusions you're reaching, here," he asked Siriom. "What do we imagine happened to bring about this ... interaction ... between the grass and the animal?" It was a measure of the Program's findings, so far, that this creature was *the* animal.

"Well, *conclusion* is a misleading word. In this case, anyway. We've been here eighteen days, and the process that we're talking about took ... no one knows how long. But a lot longer than eighteen days. For one thing, the grass doesn't attack the animals. The one animal we know about, anyway. And we know that it attacked a rover. So we can argue that there had to be something else, something that threatened the grass. *That appeared to be a threat* is a better way to say that. Otherwise, why would it waste energy evolving a defense capability?"

"But no one believes that it was a cognitive process, right? We don't think the grass said, *we have to defend ourselves?* And then did something about it?"

"It's hard to say yes or no. Evolution isn't that kind of thing. In a species like, say, *us*, it approaches that. We needed a cure for the epidemic, and we put resources in place, studied it, experimented, managed to slow it and then stop it. We don't claim that behavior for other species ... any that we know of ... yet. But the analogy to what we're seeing here would be if we'd let the disease alone, done nothing, and only humans that happened to have immunity ... if that had even been possible ... would have survived. And they and their offspring would have begun attacking whatever it was that was killing them, so to speak, using that immunity. A microbe, like the one that caused the epidemic, sharp leaves and cooperation with some kind of herbivore, here. We think. We haven't found that original threat, yet. Or them. Could have been many."

"Doesn't that mean ... the fact that you haven't found it ... that it had to be so long ago that there aren't any surface remains? Fossils? Tracks in, say, sand? Or hardened in mud?"

"You'd think so. And we don't know if there are any or not. Only a tiny part of the surface has had attention from probes and rovers. The rest is satellite images, and if the herbivores were small, or ... soft bodied, for example, it'd be sheer chance that there'd be evidence of them."

"Wouldn't the plants evolve different behavior, once the threat was gone?"

"Okay, two things, there. One, If we were talking about humans, maybe. *Bad things gone, stop wasting energy.* But it doesn't work that way for most species. If what we think about this pair of beings is even close to right, they're mutually dependent. If ... and this is definitely *if* ... each one needs the other one and there aren't alternative sources of food, water, etc., then neither side has any incentive to change. Even with the original threat no longer a thing."

She paused. "Oh, and we don't have *any* empirical data to prove that there *was* another threat. Maybe the rodents were originally eating the live grass, and they stopped doing it. And the grass stopped attacking them. For some other reason."

"You said there were two things."

"Two, we don't know if the threat *is* gone. It could be a seasonal ... phenomenon. An animal, a bird, maybe. That only comes around at a specific time of year. Something that can be driven away or even killed by the grass spiking it. And ... if that was happening, maybe the bodies of the attacking species were there, for a while, and then something *else* came and ate *them*? So they're not around for us to examine?"

"A scavenger, coming to clean up the battlefield? I like it."

"Just be sure to say *We don't know.* And we may or may not come back here. That's star one, planet one for this trip. Day after tomorrow, we're going off to look at a whole different neighborhood."

===

Late afternoon in the Virginia countryside. MacIntyre sat back in his chair, out on the big porch, thinking about next steps. A plan, in his perception of the word, was a desired outcome, supported by a series of things that had to happen for the result to be realized. In a corporate world, he might have made a reasonable project manager, if he could have separated the customer's needs from his own.

His desired outcome now was a return to positive cash flow for himself. Getting a job wasn't even on the list of possible approaches. He was aware that he'd never really worked a day in his life, in any traditional sense of the word "work." So getting a job was not in the plan. Rather, he wanted a gradual return to the idea that wandering around in outer space could be promoted and possibly accomplished by enthusiastic entrepreneurs, people with more money than ethics. And that people like himself could return to making money off fluctuations in stock, driven by the entrepreneurs' attempts. Before the epidemic, that had been possible, although with a lot of time spent talking, thinking, talking some more, and occasionally taking concrete action, inside or outside the law.

Back then, space projects had been excellent subjects for that kind of thing, involving buy low, sell high opportunities, rumor spreading, judicious bribery, backing the right political candidates when necessary ... all the skills that were required for living a lifetime of not really producing a thing except reasonable amounts of money, skimmed off the top of unreasonable amounts thereof owned by many others. He'd been good at it, back when circumstances were in place to permit that approach to work. His only real goal now was to return things - or a part of things - to an era where he could live that way again. And he had ideas about that.

===

"All hands ... Note that we'll be receiving an uncrewed utility vessel shortly. No cargo will be exchanged, but reports and brief personal comms can be transmitted. If you wish to send personal notes, the following restrictions apply. One message per staff member, one hundred characters or less, not counting recipient's international comm address. Send messages to Comms office by ..."

What would I say? Anna thought. "Folks: we did good things, found good stuff. Love, Anna." She opened a general message file and typed that in. It was short of the limit, so she added "Found some exciting things*!*" She fired that off to the communication officer, along with her Father's message address. *Filing reports, again. My favorite thing.*

As she finished that, one of the "bridge" crew - the military people who ran the ship - stuck the upper half of his body in the door. He'd been pulling himself along, giving essentially the same piece of information to each of the science people: "We're about to shift to the third planet. Secure yourselves, please." This was pointless for the majority of the personnel on board. They were almost all buckled in somewhere, watching the ship's various instruments, looking at screens, and waiting for initial data from star number three. But still, someone might have forgotten, so the "fasten your seat belts" messages were delivered in person.

Not, thought Anna, *that there's anything that could happen that being belted would help ... but ... an order is an order until you are strong enough to disobey.* Her father had given her a collection of Rudyard Kipling's short stories when she was old enough to enjoy well-written fiction by an imperialist tool. "Being on the wrong side of nearly everything doesn't always lead to incoherence," he'd said. "Even Caesar could coin a good phrase."

The star's random name, assigned by the Science lead, was a random Earth toponymic, selected from an equally random set of candidates and prefixed by "Neo." Once research was completed, the team was welcome to replace the name with something else, but for starters, it got a tag automatically. This one, the second star of their mission, was initially "NeoCorfu." Anna remembered a subsequent conversation in which Siriom had said that naming a planet after the center of a 1920's fascist diplomatic success wasn't a great way to start off an analysis. *Full of surprises, that girl!* Anna had thought.

===

"So ..." Greene said. She looked around at the crew. "We've got another one-planet system, here, and so we can team people up, if that makes sense, or we spread things out. How about we get Anna to do the probes and rovers on potential sites, as soon as there's anything to work with. And Siriom, would you like to work with the orbital units? You didn't get a chance to do much of that, right?"

"Not much, no. That would be fine."

"Carolyn, you've got the experience there. How about you and Siriom throw the satellites around?"

"Good."

Carolyn Taylor was an old hand with the above-atmospheric equipment. She'd been on two missions already, with a total of eight evaluated planets. Greene was interested in training up a replacement, since Carolyn could easily be swapped into another ship if someone had, say, another auto accident.

"All right, now Steve, will you summarize what we've got on this system?

"Sure. So ... what we've jumped into is a one-planet system, a fairly young star with a single, apparently rocky planet orbiting it. No obvious satellites, no moons, nothing. With the very early data we've got, I'd say it's *young*. And my colleague agrees with me." He looked at another man floating nearby. "Right, colleague?"

"No basis to disagree, so far. Some atmospheric moisture, yes. So there's water, somewhere. But still, I think it's a young place, for sure." Ari Pine was born in Morocco, but he'd been in the PR for most of his life, learning first the meteorology of Earth, then the new field of making educated guesses about the weather on other planets.

"Okay," Greene said. "None of that adds up to a very exciting planet. What we need to find out, right off the bat, is what the water situation might be. If there is any. I don't want to use up no-return hardware until we know there's something for it to look at. Objections?" There weren't any.

So, Carolyn and Siriom, get your orbiters out there. Let's see if there are any jade idols."

===

MacIntyre disliked quite a large number of things. He wasn't a list-maker, but if he had been, the list of entities he deprecated would have been substantial. It would have included specific governments and specific political parties, specific individuals and professions, kinds of food, religions in general, and most journalists.

In that latter case, the exceptions were those who were willing to talk with him off the record, then go away and write articles that supported MacIntyre's world view in whatever form it was currently taking. This afternoon, he was having one of those conversations with a political columnist. The gist of it was that MacIntyre ("a noted financial figure") considered international reaction to the epidemic as over-rigorous, that the task of securing humanity's health from nasty space bugs was beyond the competence of governments, and that private ventures should be allowed back into space.

The resulting article would include a specific comment, credited to "a well-regarded financial advisor," and asserting that the Starship program was of benefit solely to the governments who were enabling it, that it had yet to turn a profit (his phrase), and that it was depriving the commercial sector of an opportunity to participate in shaping the future. The writer thanked him for his time, promised to let him know when the article would be published, and signed off. There were still, of course, business schools and journals; he knew a few whose editors would at least read the draft. It was all in a day's work for the writer.

And that was the way MacIntyre looked at it, too. One more box to check off his list, if he'd had one.

===

"What we want to do, here, is to get a network of cameras crisscrossing the surface and building up a mesh of images. You've seen the results, last planet. Here's the method behind them." Carolyn gestured at a screen. The surface of the planet was shown in a long view, one side entirely visible. She clicked a checkbox, and curves around the planet appeared. "Those are the orbits. You've seen all that. On the other hand, maybe this isn't familiar." She put a finger on a touch pad and moved it slightly. The equidistant lines began to concentrate, making the center of their pattern follow her touch. "The more we concentrate the units on a small area, the more comparable data we get. And it's time-tagged, since each orbiter runs at a slightly different altitude and an equally differing speed. You try it."

"And there's no way I can crash them? Into each other?" Siriom had a horror of damaging gear.

"If that happens, it means something is wrong with the algorithm. It's supposed to keep us from doing that."

"All right." She looked closely at the image. "What about ... there?" Her finger touched the screen near a visibly patterned part of the surface. The lines converged there. "What would I see, if I did that? Imagery, I mean."

"You'd see a single image of the surface there, about ten or so kilometers across. The way the settings are now. And it would be constantly updating. As one of your orbiters hands off to another."

"I can pick just some of them, right?"

"Yes. On a planet like this, you probably won't get much additional information, beyond two or three of your satellites at once, pointed at one place. A city would be different. But there are none of those here ... unless they're underground."

===

Three "days" of imaging ensued. Siriom and Taylor spread their net widely at first, then began narrowing it as possibly interesting areas suggested themselves. At one point, Taylor, working at the next station over from Siriom, said "Have a look at this little amusement park." Her station sent an image to Siriom's.

"Ooo. That's kinky." It was a square kilometer of the surface, and It exhibited some extreme relief, with conical formations rising up sharply, tapering to points. Siriom pointed to one with her cursor. "That looks like a bell. Or a white chocolate candy." She paused, deciding how informal she could be with her more experienced colleague. *What the hell?* she thought. "Or a breast."

Taylor grinned. The boredom was having an effect. "And look at these ... pizza tray things." Some of the cones rose up and were then capped off by roughly circular brown disks. Parts of the level surface were that same brown, and other parts were the light gray, but flowing as if they'd been washed down from their parent cones. "Oh, yeah!" The image was briefly obscured by a small whirlwind, picking up portions of the brown and gray sands and carrying them away. "That's a rope tornado."

"More confirmation that this place has an atmosphere, at least."

"And a sense of humor. That wind came in from the east. Let's go back over its track and see if it exposed anything." They did. The surface continued to show a consistently chaotic face, showing more of the pillars, with or without caps, areas of sand, areas of bedrock, more sand, more pillars ... and then, as the instrumentation showed a general decline of elevation, they stopped in their metaphorical tracks.

A different kind of mound appeared, rising to twice the elevation of the others. Instead of being polished by the wind, its surface was a mixed batch of gray and brown stripes, running to the top. At the bottom, the base showed evidence of erosion channels, running away from the feature. And the top of it was a dish, filled with some kind of liquid. "Water or something like it!" Siriom said.

"Yes. And ... I'll be damned if it isn't steaming!"

===

The next steps were taken in parallel. Anna was tasked with flinging a pair of probes - the flying observation vehicles - down onto the area. Geology people were called away from their macro investigations. The microbiologist was placed on alert. "We've got a hot spring, here!"

All the various science teams involved in the effort clustered along one row of Level Two. On Level Three, the launch people stood by. Doctor Greene, clinging to a hand grip above the workstations, was moderately pleased. At least this planet wasn't going to be a complete bust.

"Anna," she said, "What's your status?"

"Nearly there. Almost surface. Five minutes, plus or minus."

"Good. What I'd like to do is have one probe slow-circling around the upper part. High enough to see down into the dish. And the other one to look around the base. See if there's anything more than just eroded rock."

"Got it."

The more senior of the geologists spoke up. "You know, I'm getting substantial *deja vu* from this. This reminds me of a formation in Yellowstone. Big dome, hot springs inside, calcium and other stuff building up the mound. As it overflows. This is *old*." This line of reasoning was carried on for a few minutes. Then Anna reported that her probes were on site.

"Going up above the dome with probe 12," she said. Screens changed. "Probe 5 closing in to look at the foot."

"Good. Anna ... " Greene was hovering over her workstation "... don't go right over it - if there are gases coming up, we want to know what they are before we run a probe through 'em. But get in, say, as far as the edges of the ... pond, or whatever it us." The imagery moved slowly under the camera. "Look at that green, mixed in with the white."

As the probe closed in, there was a general expression of enthusiasm. What they were seeing was a soup kettle, gently bubbling a broth of what might be water and a batch of what might be ... things ... appearing as green masses. "Algae!" "Maybe moss!" "Or ... embryonic ... things!"

===

And that, to most of the group's disappointment, was that. The orbital imagery turned up clusters of these hot springs and their mineral mounds, lying around the planet's equator and extending north and south from it in a belt nearly six thousand kilometers wide. Once you knew what you were looking for, they were easy enough to identify from orbit. And the bulk of them did look like features in Yellowstone National Park.

They called the star system NeoTarawera, with a bow to a nineteenth century New Zealand earthquake event. The orbital units were recalled, and the still unnamed green things continued to carry on living their extremophilic lives. The humans prepared to close out this star's log and move on to the next target. Anna suggested that the report include a recommendation for a return visit in approximately five hundred thousand standard years. "To see how things are going."

===

There were two men from the program leadership. One of them asked an engineer, "Michelle? Où est Ingénieur Untermann?"

"I'm sorry, monsieur. Niels is ... not here." The other party looked blank. "Ich meine, er is nicht ... ach, nein..." She had her phone in hand, and she spoke to it, then held the screen up for the other party to see. It said "Il est muté. À l'installation du logiciel."

"Danke." He turned to his colleague." The engineer says that Untermann has ... moved ... to another task. Task group, I mean. He is reassigned."

"Ah." The other man looked at the engineer and said "Ich

verstehe. Wissen Sie vo?"

"Nein, mein Herr. Es tut mir leid."

"We'll need to talk to personnel. See what the *raison* was. And where."

===

They reached their third star, made their third entry into a system, and took an initial inventory of its planets, planetoids, et al. "Well," Doctor Greene said, "this one wins on planet count, anyway. Otherwise ... maybe not so much."

The star had, in fact, three planets. The first of them was a rocky, overheated lump, not unlike Mercury, back in the good old Sol System. The version here was even less welcoming. "This is a sad situation, here," said Greene. "Orbital eccentricity. The light it gets is all over the map, the poles never get any at all. It's taken a beating from impacts. And there's really nothing in the way of an atmosphere. Some hydrogen, maybe. A little helium, perhaps. But nothing to write home about. Even though we do, in fact, have to write home about it."

She looked at the team, hanging onto straps around the Second Level work area. "Anybody interested in more than a scanner mapping, maybe one orbiter?"

Steve Merrill spoke up. "To quote E.B. White, I say it's spinach, and I say the hell with it." Of the assembled multitude, only Siriom laughed.

Greene said, "To quote Rudyard Kipling, explain, explain, explain."

"You mean about the planet or the quote?"

"Either."

"The planet is a waste of time. As you said, it's even less likely to have anything of interest to this mission than Mercury would. And the quote is from a nineteen-twenties cartoon. A child's looking at a plate of something, and she says that line to her mother."

"Oh. Anybody else?" No one had any other input. "Fine. How about the second one? It's farther out, probably not all that hot, in the temperature sense of the word. Ari?"

"Agreed," Ari Pine said. "It's cooler, but man, it's a rock. Might have been a capture, maybe not long after the star formed, you know, it got grabbed as it went by. But it's showing us nothing in terms of atmosphere, let alone weather. And no volcanism. Right, Steve?"

"Right."

"Other opinions?" Nothing.

"Okay, two down. How about the gas ball? Planet number three, Anna? Carolyn? Siriom?"

Carolyn Taylor said "Anna? You took a long look at it with Phil. What do you think?"

"Phil and I talked about it, and we think it might have one or more planetoids orbiting it..." People's heads turned. "...In a few million years. It's a gas giant, it's got what might make a nice moon - again, since we're quoting things - when we are dust, when we are dust. Not on this trip, though."

"Tony, what do you say?"

The ship's Captain shook his head. "You're the experts. We ..." He waved an arm at his people. "... just sail the ship."

"All right, then. All that remains is to give it a name and move along. Suggestions?"

Captain DiBiasi raised his hand. "NeoAegospotami. The battle that sank the Athenians."

===

This time, Cordell and Gorsky were together, and O'Neill was on-line. "So," Gorsky said, "the latest Technical Group report seems to have cleared one thing up, at least. The suggestion that someone was drinking on a Starship was exaggerated. It was a software engineer at the European Facility, strictly ground-based, and it doesn't sound as though he was being belligerent or dangerous. Just a bit irresponsible. They transferred him to deployment, though. Updating the Ships' Location software, when there's something to update."

"That's nice," O'Neill said. "I must be out of touch with that kind of personnel work. I have a vague memory that one deals with dependency issues via counseling rather than boredom."

"Meg, you had a take on that, I think?"

"Yes. The statement that the Group issued was very straightforward. The detail communications were a little more confused. There were different departments looking into it, different ideas about *what* they were looking into. The transfer was very quick, and I wasn't able to get at any documents ... nothing except his salary switching from one department budget to another. Overall, I don't get the sense ... of it having been taken very seriously.

"All right. I can't see anything especially ... dramatic ... in it, anyway. *Yet*, I should say." Gorsky shifted gears. "Now, do we have anything more on S339? Otto, anything coming your way?"

"No, sadly. As you, Captain..." He nodded at Meg. "... were able to confirm for me, the people in Washington don't see him as anything but an unpleasant old capitalist. He does owe a law firm a great deal of money. That surfaced when I spoke briefly with an acquaintance down there. I'm afraid we'll have to be patient. If he's doing the kinds of things we think he is, it'll come up, somehow."

===

The fourth star was even more of a "Come back when you grow up, girl" situation. None of the crew knew anything about Bobby Vee or any other mid-twentieth century pop singers, but this star system was very much a case of *formin' ain't easy, atmosphere's tough*. It had a single dwarf planet and a system full of smaller bodies. Two of them, well out from the star, appeared to have recently - in an astronomic sense of the word - collided with each other. Nothing but the dwarf appeared even worthy of a look.

Anna and Siriom paired up for a Probes-and-Rover drop, after the orbital investigation showed a series of linear features, scattered around along the equator. It turned up visible fault lines, emphasized by darker rock along the south side of a line, with lighter, sedimentary rock on the north. Greene, who had substantial geologic background, thought they were mostly shearing faults. "Looks like aggregate rock formations in the south, and sandstone north of it. And they don't like each other." None of the imagery showed any indication of life. Siriom tracked the imagery along the fault, stopping when a cone appeared, rising a hundred or so meters above the otherwise flat surface. It sat directly south of the line, with evidence of flows to the north. Further along, an oval area of darker surface appeared. "Old impact?" Anna asked.

"Likely," said Greene. They looked further from the long shear line. A low mountain range cut diagonally across the display. It appeared to be granitic, showing areas of coarse pink rock, butted up against similar light gray formations. "Volcanic flows ... or something like them."

Anna looked up. "Turning off image analysis." There was a pause. "Ick," she said. The raw images were all blacks and grays, under a solid cloud layer. The clouds themselves were glowing orange on their northern edges, as they disappeared beyond the planet's edge. "Looks like hell," she said.

"It does." Doctor Greene leaned back from the display. "You know what else looks like this? Venus."

"I was just thinking that," said Siriom.

As an experiment, they sent a single probe - no rovers - into the atmosphere. The assembled Science team watched as it descended. "Temperatures rising," said Carolyn Taylor. "Getting hotter ... Oh, dear!" The monitoring displays either pegged on their high sides or cratered. "Trying recovery ... trying ... nope. Probe is gone."

"Well," said DiBiasi, "Look at the bright side. Think of all the other hardware we *didn't* lose."

Greene smiled. "What do you say we go look at that last star? And then head on home."

Steve Merrill smiled. "Agreed. How about calling this one NeoInfernum?"

Seven: Going Home

All was quiet. Nothing, obviously, was brooding over the face of the waters. There weren't any. There was a moderately bright star, and two planets orbited around the star and simultaneously around each other. Without any prelude, a rectangular object appeared, becoming extant where there had been nothing.

"In orbital position," said a voice, speaking within the object. "In planned orbit. Planetary inventory group, hit the deck." The last star on the Bolton's list of targets was out there, and task one was to determine what kind of planets it had to offer, if any. Anna and Siriom emerged from their cabins and headed to the working level. "We're betting on two, right?" Anna asked.

"Right. At least that's what Doctor Greene said. And it's roughly Sun-equivalent, so maybe ... I don't know, little green men?"

"Or at least some jade idols."

By the time they'd gotten set up in their work stations, the word was out. The star did, in fact, have two planets. They were of roughly the same size as Earth, and the planetary mechanics person was being very enthusiastic. There was a chance that they were binary.

Doctor Greene floated up, talking to her comm device. "Are they orbit-clearing, though? One of 'em isn't a satellite of the other? Okay, let me know." She pulled herself over to Anna's area. "We don't know for sure what the worlds are, yet - but it's kind of academic. Either way, we want to image 'em up, see if there's any compelling reason to visit one before the other."

"They're pretty much the same size," Siriom said. "Visually, anyway. And both at the same solar distance, give or take."

"Right. The planet boys say about 1.4 AU. Nearly Mars' distance. So how about you guys split 'em between you? Pick one each, and I'll get the notification paths set."

This latter was a process step, defining which crew members got the most recent information on something, as it happened. In the case of a two-planet system and basic values, it wasn't critically important; almost everybody would get any initial news. Then, as data accumulated, it would become useful to route data to the crew most likely to need it.

===

Brussels, as a city in general, had suffered. Throughout most of its history, it had been at least a target for some army or other, if not actually a victim. More recently, it had suffered from a less physically threatening invasion, but certainly an existential one. The tourism boom of the twenties had flooded it - as it had most other western European cities - with people from elsewhere. Now, the bloom was off the lily or the rose or whatever vegetation it had been on, and the days were gone when every intersection offered a mix of local and overtly non-native eating places. Especially around the universities, there were now a smaller number of ordinary eateries, plus a similar group called "bars" in a range of languages. The cuisines and drinks varied with a perceived market ("What do people want?"), a preference on the part of owners and managers ("This is how we do it."), or a clinging to an older set of factors ("This is what we did, twenty years ago.").

One of the latter places sat on a traffic circle, where a smaller street met the Avenue de l'Université. It had an odd structure, given that it occupied differing amounts of frontage on a side street and on the Avenue. It looked bent, like a re-used cardboard box.

It was close to 1600 hours, and the bar's only patrons were a man and a woman. He appeared to be in his thirties, and he had a look, everything taken together - size, hair, clothing, absence of beard or mustache - that hinted at *professional guy*. Seeing him, you might guess that he'd been a bit healthier a few years before, been in slightly better shape, been, maybe, a little more self-confidant than he was now. His name was Niels Untermann.

The woman was probably ten years older. If you saw her on the street, she might have been almost any kind of local. She looked urban without being especially urbane, old enough to be a mother but without any visible indication of it. Seeing her, there in the bar, you might or might not have altered that perception. There weren't a lot of other indicators.

She was sitting across from Untermann, saying nothing and listening to him with apparent interest. What he was saying was related to his recent removal from a software development role and his being pushed into a quality assurance job. He was speaking in German, and the gist of it was that he was unhappy with the situation, and he was looking for a way to express his displeasure. He was speaking quite softly, even though there was no one else in the place.

When he'd finished, the woman said a few sympathetic things. Then she began talking at greater length about a way he might be able to leave the program while still having a source of funds. Forty minutes later, they left the bar and walked away in different directions.

===

Aboard The Bolton, there was some discussion of the two planets. Were they both, in fact, planets? Did one of them constitute a satellite of the other one? Or were they really a twin planet pair? The debate was moving toward the latter idea, and it was finalized when the math showed clearly that the barycenter, that difficult concept, the single point around which both of them orbited, lay outside both of them. They were actually two *planets*, not a planet and a *moon*.

The environmental status team, the group that assessed the likelihood of life forms, was moving toward a *not-likely* assessment, although without yet having orbited either one. Still, they were able to assert that planet 1 was a hot one, probably with an oxidizing atmosphere, not an especially life-friendly place. Planet 2, spending more of its time further from the star, was less hostile, though still not a paradise. There were conversations about whether the distance from the star for either candidate was enough to expect life.

The call, finally, belonged to Doctor Greene. "It doesn't matter what we *want* to find. It's a resources call. We have orbiters, we have probes, we've got rovers ... and we can use them here or save 'em for later. But for this mission, this *is* later." She looked around. "Mutually orbiting planets are rare, we think. But not unheard of. Hell, Pluto and Charon, back home, are MO. The question is: Do we expend drones and rovers on this duo, or don't we?"

There was some back and forth. But, like a pendulum winding down its motion, the decision wobbled back and forth a bit, then ended up with a non-binary solution.

"So we put satellites around both of 'em. From that data, we pick a pair of sample sites on each one. Drop a probe and - if it merits it - a rover on each of those sites. And we look around. We switch to the other planet and do that same thing. If, in the course of that, anything stands up and waves at us - or shoots at us - we re-think our approach. Otherwise, we go with what we've got, off-planet the rovers and probes, call in the satellites, and go home. What do you say?" Nobody disagreed. That "home" word was compelling.

===

"MacIntyre." It was late and he was tired, but he was also willing to speak with the caller. It didn't take long. When it ended, he made a note for himself, writing it on a small pad of paper. Then he started getting ready for bed. The note, laying there on his side table, just said "buy stock."

===

Siriom watched imagery from an orbiter as it passed across the hot surface of planet one. If you cleared your mind of analysis and relied solely on reaction, it was kind of pretty. A flat, gray plain showed a network of cracks or channels, mostly lighter in color, wandering and looping around. A few of them had small sections of black. As the orbiter moved, making a lateral pass around the north-central plain, there had suddenly been a change. She'd grabbed the image as a still frame, and was staring at it.

The quilted surface ended abruptly, giving way to a rock-strewn area, making an arc across the lower right quarter of the picture. Whatever the rocks were, they appeared black on the shadowed eastern side, bright on the other one. It made them look almost chromed. She zoomed in to the point where they became pixelated. Although it made an attractive image, there wasn't the slightest hint of biology, technology, or - for that matter - even symbology. It was a desert plain on the surface of a hot, dry, airless planet. She sighed and went back to watching the surface scroll by.

===

"Launch Chamber, two and four programmed. Let 'em go, please."

"Right, Anna. Stand by ... two and four on their way down."

Anna looked over toward Siriom. "Should be a couple of hours. Lunch?"

===

"So ..." said Doctor Greene, "... analysis?"

"There is ... a lot of hot rock down there. And not much else." Steve Merrill was wearing his unenthusiastic face. "Maybe I'm ... what? Hastening to judgment? But ..."

"Second that emotion," Siriom said. "Anna?"

"Can't disagree. A lot of baked granite. Hot rock, as Steve put it."

"Carolyn?"

"Lemme outta here."

"All right. Let's go have a look at planet two, shall we?"

===

A planet is not easy to parse, at least from the far-orbit where the Starships stayed. To understand a world in any useful way requires a closer look, and that was the role of the orbiters. These small and recoverable devices were flung down toward each planet the team visited. Once there, they began looking at the surfaces below, usually beginning with the apparent equator, then moving up or down around the circumference of the current target.

Another thing they were able to do was confirm or deny assumptions that may have been made. In the current case, they confirmed the idea that biology was not obvious. But they also moved the "interesting" measure up the scale. The planet didn't just have a rocky surface, it was scenic.

"If you can do without trees, this would be a nice place to hike around." Anna said. "It's had volcanism, it must have had weather. Those mountains didn't get that way just by themselves." She was looking at a vast stripe of rocky territory, running diagonally up across the planet's center line. New Mexico came to mind, along with places in the Rocky Mountains, Colorado, Montana.

"It went through some things," Doctor Greene said. "Look at this." Her screen showed a wide range of rounded mountains, divided by what seemed to be absolutely flat valleys, some of them wider than the mountains were tall. "That would be a tiring place to hike around."

"Or crawl, or hop, or gallop."

"Thirsty, too," said Siriom. Nothing I'm looking at is showing me water."

"And needless to add, we're not getting emissions of any kind. No visible settlements, no evidence of exploitation."

"But," Anna said, "I think we want to put a probe and rover combination down there somewhere. Maybe in one of those flat places. Just to see."

"Ari? Want some ground-level weather data?"

"Yes, please. We don't see anything blowing around - sand, or anything - but it would be nice to confirm it." Meteorology had already determined that there was an atmosphere, not a human-friendly one, but at least a mix of typical atmospheric gases.

"All right. Anna and Siriom - put a couple of probe/rover pairs on that big, flat space. For one thing, we ought to know what that sand used to be, before it became sand. And why it's not still up on those mountainsides where it belongs."

"Great," said Anna.

"Oh, and get Ari his air data."

"Thanks," Ari said. "It's lonely, being an air head."

===

"Well ... we can tell Ari that, no, there's no breeze blowing. And the stuff on the ground isn't quite what I'd call sand." Siriom was looking at the tightest closeup the rover camera could supply. It was almost a microscope, if you could imagine one on the end of a flexible arm, moved around by a joystick in a vessel outside the atmosphere of the planet. The ground cover was dust, yellow dust. The question of its essence - was it something worn off much larger rocks and into its extremely small, powdery grains, or was it dust to begin with - was not easily determined. Jamming a pointed collection stick down into the surface got almost nowhere. A centimeter or two below, there was a harder layer of rock, and chipped off samples showed a different color and what was probably a crystalline nature.

There were also scattered places where the underlying rocks showed through, appearing as linear features, a meter or two in length. Looking off into the distance, the plain ended in a range of higher ground, lower than the mountains elsewhere, and coated in a gray dust, clearly different from the material they'd been examining.

"So,..." Anna began.

"So." said Siriom.

"So," said Doctor Greene, "I say we pack our virtual bags and go home. I've looked at all the ... dirt... I can stand for this trip."

"What about a name?" DiBiasé asked?

"NeoOlduvai? A place where something might happen, eventually?"

===

In the EU launch facility, Untermann was ostensibly updating a suite of tests. When run, they poked the Location shift software in a large number of ways, watching for its response and recording the results.

"Poking" didn't imply any changes in the Shifter software itself. All it did was simulate the information that the Shifter might receive from humans, from its own hardware, and from its own results. If it were to be given good data from a specific test and didn't react as its design said it would, that would be a defect. Likewise, if if got bad data and tried to use it anyway, that was also an error. Either one got logged, along with all the things that were going on when it happened, and the software engineers would have another bug to fix.

Untermann had been one of those engineers. He'd fixed many bugs over the course of the project. Some of them had been in his own code. And he had code in the new version. He had a good sense of how that code was supposed to work, and he was confident that it would pass its tests. Especially if he knew what the tests would be looking for and - more importantly - *not* looking for. He felt slightly better about the transfer. Somewhere along in his education, he'd run into an old Latin tag, *Quis custodiet ipsos custodes?,* that is,"Who guards the guards?" Suddenly, it meant much more to him. *Who tests the tests?* he thought.

===

The trip back was as apparently as simple-seeming as usual. The Starship crew did their work recovering the orbiters. Greene and the rest of the science group began collecting their thoughts, data, and perceptions. Things were stowed, reports began to be written. And without any serious fanfare, the ship's crew activated the Location shift unit. There were two, either one serving as a backup for the other. There hadn't been a malfunction on any of the Starships since the program launched, but ... you always want backup.

The navigation officer fastened herself in at the unit's keyboard. The PR base and this mission's stars were each selectable options. She chose *North America Base* as a destination, ordered a quick self-test, and then typed "operate." A few messages, largely composed of digits, appeared, and ... the display showed *North America Base. Earth orbit.*

She touched the communications switch and said "We're home."

===

Meg Cordell and her partner, Larry, were creatures of habit. Both of them got up and out of the house in the morning. Meg's job in Intelligence Branch required her physical presence for the vast majority of the things she did. Larry's tasks were less national than individual. He counseled unhappy, uncertain, or confused young people; neither of them did the kind of things that lent themselves to working from home.

In the evenings, they'd draw a line between career and fun. Both were reasonably good cooks, and they also enjoyed putting some of their government salaries back into the city's large and diverse restaurant and entertainment economy. Regardless, though, they routinely watched "The National." It was the Republic's primary end-of-day news wrap up and editorial program. On this particular night, the third segment was an update on the Starship program.

"Ah," said Meg. "This'll be interesting."

The segment began with video of the NeoFrisia Planet 2 "rodent" and its "grass." The show's host explained the discoveries and the fascinating evolutionary questions they raised. A guest from the Starbase Flynn staff talked about the techniques and technologies, and she walked the viewer through some imagery, including video of a shuttle launch from the PR base ("Silent, no smoke and flame, look at the deer herd over there, paying no attention"). She talked about the international nature of the program and showed footage of the second North American ship, currently nearing completion. The presenter asked if had a name yet.

"Not yet, but it'll follow the current pattern, naming the ships after prominent socialist figures."

"Living people?"

"No, people involved in the development of socialism. The ship operating out of the Republic's Starbase Flynn, for example, is the Virginia Bolton. She was prominent in nineteenth and twentieth century socialism in Argentina."

"Oh, yes. And I recall the naming of the Starbase here, Elizabeth Flynn, am I right?"

"Right. Elizabeth Gurley Flynn. She was an early twentieth century American socialist figure. And let me say that the importance of naming ships and bases after these people is to keep everyone focused on the international and especially the *public* nature of the program. The epidemic revealed the importance of that, but it goes all the way back to the beginnings of for-profit healthcare. It's based on scientific work that involves all the world's people, all of the life here, and it has to be an effort of the people in general, not something concerned with profit."

"As we've seen," the host said. The screen displayed a montage of opium-based patent medicines from the nineteenth century. "Well, thank you very much for joining us, and we'll be looking forward to further developments from the grasses and the rodents of NeoFrisia Planet two. I'm Jackie Beyer for The News."

"Laying it on a little thick, don't you think?" Larry asked.

"I hope not. I hope people take that to heart." That was as much as Meg could say, even to her partner, but the one picture Security Branch had of MacIntyre was in her mind.

Larry said nothing more. He interpreted her remark - the thing she'd said, and the tone of her voice - as representing a reality he'd experienced before. *There's a thing she can't talk about, and I'll probably see it in the news, later.*

===

This time, after the shuttle ride down to the base, the crews did get a lift back from the pad, in a small green truck, sitting in the back like infantry. It had "PR - FB" painted on the doors. "That means Field Branch," Anna said. "The PR army. The police are the SB. Like the people who were dealing with the moose." Siriom was partly successful in pretending to be interested.

They spent the remainder of the day stretching, lying down, getting up to put some of their gear away, lying down, having a meal, and doing more or less the same thing, ending with sleep. The next day they woke, more or less in the morning, calibrated themselves to concepts like morning, night, time of day, and so on, and after a bit more food and some coffee, they went for a walk. After ten minutes, they found a bench and sat down.

"I'll bet this is going to be the hardest part of missions," Siriom said. "Getting back, sitting around, walking around, sitting around. And reminding yourself that you've got leave to think about. Vacation. Doing things."

"I agree." Anna stretched her legs out and flexed the gastrocnemius muscles. They were returning to their duty, but they hurt, less than they had yesterday, but they hurt. "Still ... a few things to be done, but then, yes, time off."

There was a quiet minute or two. Siriom was looking straight ahead, across the central base road and out into the woods. Anna, instead, was looking directly at her colleague's profile. Very dark hair framed it, partly covering the ear. Her eyebrows, equally dark, drew an arch over her eyes, each one ending almost exactly at the nose bridge. It was a long nose, making a clear, triangular shape, not quite pointed, but defined. It would have made her expression severe, except for high cheek bones that were always evident, even more so with a smile to highlight them. Anna had never seen images of the parents, but she guessed that most of Siriom's genome had come from her Sikh mother.

An image of her own face came to mind and with it the notion that they were, herself and her colleague, not very much alike in appearance. Anna was almost stereo-typically Irish. Her hair wasn't precisely red, but certainly red-blonde. She had a round face, blue eyes, almost invisible light-colored eyebrows. And she was a bit shorter than Siriom. *Diversity*, she thought. And then, noting Siriom's thousand-yard stare, *I wonder what she's thinking?*

"Do you have a plan for going on leave?" she asked. "Part of it or all of it?" Siriom looked down at her feet.

"I ... don't,, really. But I wanted to talk about it."

"Me, too," said Anna, surprising herself.

"It's been a while since I ... needed to talk about things ... other than weird grass and publishing papers. But." She paused.

"But?"

"Would you want ... would you like to go somewhere? Together, again, I mean?" She turned her head and looked right at Anna.

"I ..." A mental switch changed state abruptly. "Yes," Anna said.

"Okay. Good. I should... say something, though."

"Okay."

"I don't really like ... men ... very much." She left that hanging.

"Well ... " Anna paused. *How do you say this?* "My ... experience ... has been with men. But ... " Siriom was looking directly at her eyes. "... I've thought about ... women. Too. And there isn't anybody ... that I'd be seeing. When I go on leave... wherever I'd go. So ... "

"So, we wouldn't necessarily have to get two rooms, you mean? Like last time?"

"Right. Yes. We wouldn't."

"Good."

There was a pause. Both of them were now looking away, elsewhere than at each other. As they sat there, an aircraft appeared and circled around the landing strip, setting up for arrival.

"We should make arrangements," Siriom said. "When should we go?"

"How about tomorrow? And where?"

"Um ... to the Capital? All I've seen there is the airport and a hotel."

"Fine. That's what I would have picked. You'll like it. It's a nice city." They locked eyes again.

"Good," Siriom said.

===

A day later, the two women were sitting, once again, on benches, this time at the airstrip. They had a reasonable amount of luggage with them, and they had two week's worth of reservation at a hotel near the Capital's center.

"Of course, " Anna said, "We need to start thinking about that dissertation. It's going to be a bit of work."

"I know. But when Doctor Greene brought it up, I realized that I don't know how this joint authorship works."

"Um ... it's just that we both do the work, do the writing, submit it together to the same group ..."

"Really? It's not just an individual effort?"

"No. Most Doctorates here are some kind of group effort. Everybody has to do a defined part of the work ... or share some part of it equally. You don't hear about individual work, all that much. People expect that there'll be a team."

"And if it's excepted, everybody gets a Doctorate?"

"Well, if everybody doing it already has a Master's. But a group can have undergrads, too, and they get their Masters' degrees, not doctorates. If the work is approved, I mean. I was part of a group like that, and I got my MS that way."

"This sounds so different than the way it works, um, elsewhere."

"I know. There are starting to be schools, though ... individual colleges, I mean ... outside the Republic. There's one in Dublin with Master's and PhD program teams in socialist theory and history."

"So, we'd be a group?"

"Sure. And maybe other people from the mission. We might get Doctor Greene to head up the committee, even."

"Wow. Amazing." She paused. "Listen. That sounds like the plane. Are you ready?"

"Oh, yes."

====

Niels was reading code. Parts of the Location shift operating system were written in an annoying interpreted language called AnaKonda - serious developers called it SnakeOil - and he gave it the same general disapproval his colleagues did. The serious coders and designers used compiled languages; in the PR, it was Cpr7, and elsewhere, another C-language descendant called CPrime. Niels could read Cpr7, but most of his experience was with CPrime.

Deep in the code, lying below the AnaKonda methods that received user input, was a set of dispatch operations. The user did something at the Location shifter console, the top layer looked at it and called one of the lower level methods. One of those lower level methods was a piece of Niels' work, *callShiftMode*. Its requirement was to accept a value and look at it. If it was anything but 1 or 0, it did nothing except display an error message. If it was 1, it called other code to initiate a location shift to a spot in the universe defined by other values already provided, and it reported that you were there. If it was 0, it did nothing at all except display the phrase "execute command received" in English and German.

Niels had been assigned to write this as a testing capability. Testers could enter an "operate" command and be assured that the user interface was sending "do it" to the shift hardware, but without actually activating it. In production, of course, this was undesirable; a Starship engineer could sit there all day, typing "operate" and nothing would happen. There were plenty of other things you might want to test but not actually trigger. So all of that code, everything that was supposed to accomplish something, used Niels' 0-return method to enable it. Once the code was installed, tested, and declared operational, the final installation command would stifle the 0-return.

Niels smiled.

====

"Dammit." MacIntyre was mildly annoyed. The first person he'd tried to contact about a new space investment group was not interested. More accurately, he was not available, having died in the epidemic. His estate was under the control of the Government of New Zealand, and it was being liquidated in steps, donating yearly portions of the assets to recovery and support groups. *Kiwis! I should have known.* He'd lost track of politics in many parts of the world, and he hadn't noted the return of a women-led, center-left government in Wellington.

"Oh, well. One down ..." He drew a line through that first name in his notebook, then sent off his standard message to the next person, a gentleman in Cape Town. *Rainbow Nation, phooey*, he thought. *But they got money.*

===

Anna and Siriom picked seats near the back of the plane. They'd be the last ones off, since they were going to the last stop, Capitol Airbase. "So, this is just our flight up here, in reverse? But with stops?" Siriom asked.

"A couple of stops. There are other people from our mission going south, too. For some of them, we'll be stopping at the Straits ... the south side of that big bridge. And then again at a city that's kind of in the middle of the lower part. Mount Pleasant Airbase."

"Mount Pleasant? Is that ... descriptive?"

"Well ... there's no mountain. I haven't been in the city, itself. There's a lot of the Republic I haven't been in. Now that I think of it."

"Secure for takeoff," said the second officer, his voice coming from a speaker. That was the extent of it; the assumption was made that if you were flying out of a government base, on a government aircraft, you knew what "secure" meant. Once they were off the ground and pointed east, the speaker had things to add, concerning flight times to the three stops. "Approximately an hour and a quarter to Straits Airbase, three quarters of an hour to Mount Pleasant Airbase, more or less the same to Capital. Add time on the ground, three hours, plus minus."

At the Straits airbase, four people got off, leaving just Anna, Siriom, and a man they knew as one of the academic team, responsible for routing basic planetary data to researchers all over the world. Then a young man got on, apparently traveling south by himself. There was a pause, and then three more passengers came in the plane's door. The first was a man apparently in his thirties, wearing a blue uniform. A women in civilian clothes was next, followed by another woman in a black uniform. The latter two seemed to be of a similar age, in their late fifties or early sixties. The uniformed man stepped aside as the women took a pair of seats together. Then he sat down, one row ahead of them.

"A police officer?" Siriom asked, *sotto voce*.

"The one in blue, yes. Remember the moose incident?" Anna said. "And I think ... black is the Intelligence people."

After a few minutes of administrative things, the usual announcements were made and the plane headed out onto the runway. After it was in the air, the black-clad person got up and walked back toward the other passengers. She nodded to the academic gentleman, said something to the other person, and then came down to where the Anna and Siriom were sitting. "Hi," she said. "You two are Starship science staff, right? On the Bolton?"

"Yes, just going on leave," Siriom said. Anna nodded.

"Great. I'm Eden Gorsky. I sit at a desk, down at the Capital, watching other people work. Occasionally, they let me get out and make a nuisance of myself. I heard that your mission found some actual living things?"

"Well, they seemed to be living. In a kind of single-minded way, but living." Anna was slightly more comfortable with the Republic's informal way of communicating.

"Wow. Very good stuff. My associate up there ..." She gestured at the other person. "... is writing something to someone, right now, but I'll get her to come and have a word with you. She does things in the Education Department. They're working up the next year's curriculum, and your find would be a big addition ... History, Science, Diplomacy ... countries working together. All that stuff."

"We'd be happy to talk. I'm Anna Grover, by the way."

"And I'm Siriom Barnes."

"A pleasure to meet you. Enjoy your leave." Gorsky turned and walked back up the aisle.

"That was interesting," Siriom said.

"Yes. I ... remember that name. She runs a branch of the Army. The Intelligence Branch. There are four Generals, I think, and she's one of them."

"Oh, my.."

"And if the person with her is who I think she is, she's Director of the Department of Education."

===

MacIntyre's list was growing. He now had four potential contributors lined up, people who would benefit from private space stuff being a thing, again. His pitch included the formation of an advocacy group and identification of more political people who'd be willing to assist - there weren't any of those politicians, so far, but none of the contacts were surprised when he didn't offer names. To the contacts, it sounded like the launch of a lobby. Of course, MacIntyre had a more sophisticated objective. The more takers he could find, the more likely they'd be to start cover businesses. The more of those there were, the more stock MacIntyre could option, then sell when the prices started to go up. He'd played this game before, and it was one of the few things he was good at.

===

The trip from the Capitol Airport - the military and government airfield - to downtown was like a tour of the primary north-south streets. The tram took you north on Republic, over a substantial freeway, and then across an open space. Siriom asked if it was a park.

"Sort of. It used to be a golf course, I guess. But now it's a park and a farmer's market space." Immediately afterward, the tracks took them by that very feature. "It's getting late in the year for it, but there are still people selling. Vegetables and so on." Anna was enjoying the tour guide role. The narrative was all geosocial, and it kept both of them focused on the moment and not the immediate future. The evening and what would happen as it ended was a sort of elephant in the room.

The tracks turned north again. "And this is Capitol Avenue. That thing up ahead? It was a sports ... stadium, I guess. But now, it's a government center. They put a roof over the stadium, and it's all offices and chambers and government spaces now."

"And this takes us downtown?"

"Yes. And we have a room in a government building ... The building's half a block long. Right in the middle of everything. Doctor Strang got it for us. It's usually full of academics or military or ... visiting firemen."

"What?"

"My father used to say that. It meant important people, I think."

"Do we qualify?"

"Apparently."

===

"All right, ladies and gentlemen, it's time to go home." The Captain of the Starship George Orwell was the first human being to hold the title of Starship Captain. That she was the first woman to do so was irrelevant to her. Maria Escobedo was here, she was in command, and that was all. Every other Starship Captain, all three of them, counting the person in charge of the still-building fourth ship, felt the same way. "Secure for Location shift," she said.

The drill was the same, across all the vessels. The Science team stopped what it was doing, and the Ship's crew did what they needed to do. The operating officer set the destination to *European Base*, did the self-test, and entered the appropriate command. There was the usual on-screen output, and then they were home.

===

Anna and Siriom got their room, along with a smiling welcome. The clerk offered them information, if they needed it, on the Capital, places to eat, and so on. Anna took the brochure gladly; she'd lived in the city for several years, but never as a tourist, and never without specific goals and deadlines. Seeing it as a visitor would be a new experience.

Their room was on the fourth floor, looking out on Capitol Avenue itself. Immediately south, there was another large green space. "Is that another ex-golf course?" Siriom asked.

"No. I remember walking through there. It's a park, but ... kind of political, too."

"For rallies or speeches?"

"I don't recall any of that. But it's a place where a whole development ... expensive apartments or condos or something ... just collapsed. Before the separation ... before they left the US. And the new government fenced it in and left it as an example, I guess. It's called Greed Park."

"It looks nice, now."

"Ten or fifteen years ago ... before I came here ... they cleaned it up. And made a real park out of it. But they kept the name."

===

Gorsky and Doctor Strang were finishing a routine call, a kind of mutual reporting, since neither one had any defined authority over the other. "Now, about the thing I mentioned," Strang said, switching his screen to a document view. "I got a verbal okay from our Science chief, and ... let's see, you met Doctor Greene, right?"

"Right," Gorsky said. The screen was displaying Siriom's resume.

"And she's on board with it. So if you can call in a favor from External Relations, I'll have a chat with her when she gets back."

"Fine. Not really relevant, but are they an item? Barnes and Grover? Kristin and I were on the same plane with them coming down."

"Could be. They've been workin' together the whole time, and this is the second leave they've done together. So yeah, I'd bet on it."

"And what's Grover's status?"

"She's OK. Resident now, and if she can get a dissertation out of this, she'll be good for Citizen. And you know, if they decided to partner up - well, she could sponsor Barnes. Kind of a fall back option."

"We probably won't need it, but nice to have. I have to go - yet another meeting - but I'll get External Relations to weigh in, and get back to you."

"Thanks. If we keep this up, we'll have all the smart kids the US has left."

===

When they'd stowed their gear - that's how they thought of it, now, having had the Starship experience - they went for a walk. Immediately outside their building Capitol Avenue presented itself as an architectural mix from at least two centuries. The buildings dated from the early twentieth to the recent twenty-first, with the former dominating. The next building north of the hotel was an example, a tiny, gray-painted brick restaurant. It had angled corners, each just big enough for a door, and there were people at tables and others at stools along a counter. There was nothing in the way of signage. "I ate there, once," Anna said. "It's kind of seafood-ish. And you can sit outside in the back."

Further along, the buildings varied among ordinary and more elaborate nineteen-hundreds styles. Some were, Anna said, really old and some were just built to look like it. On the other side of the street, one or two of the structures had been retro-fitted with large upper-story windows.

"Are those apartments?" Siriom asked.

"I'm not sure. Some of them, probably. Some offices, too, I bet. " One of them, with a plain gray front, said *The Ark*. That's a music place. Performance space, I mean. We should see who's playing."

"Great."

They walked on to the end of the block. Across Capitol, there was a large restaurant, wrapping around the north-west corner. "That's a place we liked to go, when we got down here," Anna said. "It's kind of Greek without being obsessive about it."

"What do you mean when you say *down here*?"

"Oh, down from the university area. It's off east, that way." She pointed. "It gets to be fewer stores and restaurants, and more government and college. Let's just walk a block that way, and then cut back."

"Great."

The sun was lighting the north side of the street. "This is Liberty," Anna said. "Liberty Street, I mean." They walked east, past a variety of food and retail businesses, all in late-nineteenth or early twentieth century buildings. They reached the end of the block. Anna stopped, waiting for an approaching tram to go by.

"What on earth is that?!" Siriom said, pointing at the Southeast corner of the intersection.

"What? Oh, that? That is a bit strange, isn't it? It was a US government office, from the nineteen-hundreds. I had the same reaction, when I saw it."

The building looked like a fortress, designed by a post-modern architect while drunk. It offered blank brick walls, topped by full windows on the recessed faces of the three upper floors. It looked like the steps up to a front porch, designed for giants and without the porch, let alone a house.

"What were they thinking?"

"Well, you know ... student riots. It was the Vietnam war, and things were touchy. So they built these ... fortresses. I guess. That's what somebody told me."

"It's from that far back? What is it, now?"

"It's all Department of Health, I think. The psychiatric group."

===

They finished a loop around the western end of downtown. Their feet were beginning to complain, so Anna suggested they take a tram to the University area, just ride it around on its loop and end up back near the hotel for lunch. "Or do you want to eat now?"

"Not unless you do. Let's go for a ride."

The tram took them east, past Fourth and Fifth streets, Separation Avenue, Rue Jean Meslier, and Barricades Street, to the end of Liberty. There it turned south on Republic. "This is the heart of the University," Anna said, indicating the structures on the left. Like the town, the college was a mix of old and new buildings. The nearest feature was a wide area of lawn and trees, crossed by a random-seeming mesh of paved walks. Beyond it, East and South, were an almost random assortment of old and new construction. They reached a cross street, "South University," and the tram turned with it. Immediately on the right, there was a long stretch of faux-Victorian architecture. "Is that a library?" Siriom asked.

"No ... well, there's a library in it. But it's the Political Science department, now. It was the law school, before we separated." *I just said 'we' separated*, Anna thought.

Eventually, the feudal architecture gave way to more recent structures, some just as unpleasant to look at. Something like a nineteenth century mansion turned out to have been the residence of the University President, before the Republic took possession. "I don't know what that is ... " Anna began, then saw a sign: *Department of Health: Hospice Care*. They passed a mixed group of academic structures, and then the tram turned north. "It's all just student housing that way. All bars and apartments. This tram line goes back through Campus, though, and takes us back downtown." And it did, going west on a street parallel to Liberty, It was called Calla Quince Brigada. When they got to Capitol, they got off.

===

"I have a question," Siriom said. They were dining at a recommended place, just called *Below*. It turned out to be a literal designation, since it was downstairs, below a large coffee shop. "Were all these street names ... original? Or did the Republic change them?"

"Somewhere, I have a kind of guidebook they gave me. It had all the cross-references between old names and new ones. I'd have to dig it out. But I remember this one, Quince Brigada. It's *Fifteenth Brigade*, in Spanish. People from the English-speaking countries who volunteered to fight in Spain. Against fascists."

"In Spain? When?"

"Um ... nineteen thirties, I think. Before World War two."

"That was before my time."

"Mine, too." Anna held up her glass. Here's to the fighters, anyway, whoever they were."

When they came up and out onto the street, Anna pointed north.

"Up that way, ..." she said, "... is one of my favorite intersections. I guess they got tired of naming things after people, and so ... the streets are called Chaos and Community." Siriom looked blank. "I asked somebody about it, and they said it was from a song ... an old band, some kind of acid rock, you know? "

"Oh. You mean without a bass player?"

===

Siriom unlocked the door to their room, and they went in. They looked at each other's eyes, and Anna shut the door. "So," she said.

"So ..."

"I assume some of my pre-existing experience will ... apply. Right?"

"Yes. There's some common things. Removing clothing, for example."

"I know that one."

===

On their third morning, Siriom paused in the act of dressing. "How ... *open* are people here with things like this?" She gestured at the room, the bed, themselves.

"What do you mean?"

"I mean ... do you ... *come out*, or do you just assume people ... will ... what? What do people think about two women. Together, I mean?"

Oh, yes, Anna thought. *She wasn't ... she didn't go to school here.* "Did you ... get any kind of talk or something about ... genders and relationships? When you came into the Republic?"

"No. I think there was supposed to be, but there wasn't time. I had to get on that plane. With you."

"And I'm glad you did, really. But, would you like a summary?"

"Please."

"In the Republic, nobody ... individuals, organizations, the government ... *nobody* ... can make any kind of decisions about someone based on gender. None."

"That sounds so reasonable, for a government."

"It does get more complicated than that. Not surprisingly. What I was told was that when they wrote their Constitution and their laws, people were conflicted over what it meant. And so they made it really explicit. The sense of it is, what people do with each other isn't anyone else's business. As long as there's consent. And as long as everybody involved is safe and comfortable. Everything from the Constitution on down is about *Safety and Comfort* - that's what matters, here. And as long as everyone - all the people involved - are safe and comfortable, then it's nobody's business but those people involved."

"I didn't know. That's ... good. Really good."

"They have a whole school curriculum to teach it to kids. Starting when they're fourteen or fifteen. It seems to work."

"I have another question."

"Yes?"

"How did I get so lucky?"

===

By the end of their first week, Anna was feeling almost at home with the Capitol; Siriom said she found it addictive. "Seriously, every time I look around, something ... different, comes up." She paused. "But I had a question, though. Are there holidays here?"

"Well, it depends on what you mean by *holiday*. You won't get in trouble for having friends over for dinner on December 25th. Or exchanging gifts. But don't call it Christmas. There are PR celebrations, though. Just really secular."

"Like what?"

"Well, Separation Day is a big thing for people ... the date the Republic formally left the US. But it isn't what I'd call a holiday, by itself. The restaurants fill up, and people take the day off, if they can. The government doesn't do anything special. On some other days, though, there's official notice. Constitution day is one. The day it was voted in by the Council. And Great Lakes day. That was when they ratified the treaty with Canada."

"With Canada?"

"Right. Canada and the Republic agreed that the PR would take over security and public safety on three of the lakes. If Canada funded the ships."

"Three of the Great Lakes?"

"Right. Lake Superior, Lake Huron, and the eastern part of Lake Michigan. The PR ... I should just say "we" ... got three warships ... little ones, frigates ... and a lot of smaller patrol boats, oh, and ice breakers. Canada pays most of the bills, and then they're free to worry about their own ... other worries, I guess."

"I didn't know that."

"I think the US wasn't happy. I don't really know all that much about it. It was kind of downplayed, I think. You know, a thing they say here ... I heard a professor say this. *Reasonable people, dealing with unreasonable ones. Another way of defining socialism.*"

"There's a lot to know. And ... we should talk about ... well, me. About being here ... permanently."

"Yes, we really should." Anna paused. "Do you want that?"

"Definitely. As long as you're part of the package."

≡≡≡

"I suppose ... " Anna began. "I suppose I really ought to let my parents know ... where I am, anyway."

"Probably. Do you want me to ... go downstairs for a bit?"

"Um, ... no. No, I think we should ... just ... be two people. In a hotel room. All right?"

"Yes. It'll be a good trial run for talking with my father."

"So, not your mother?"

"Let's just say ... that she'll be ... more ..." Siriom shook her head. "... something. I don't know what. But something. She's always something."

"All right, then. We'll catch my people on their evening walk, probably." She picked up her phone and selected *Father* from her contacts.

===

Liscannor was a bit gray. The usual overcast for this time of year was augmented by some mist, but the residents were used to it. Dr. and Mrs. Grover were, as Anna thought, taking their walk. The house was behind them, across the road, and ahead was Liscannor Bay. The homes on the other side were invisible, but the hills behind still stood out. The father's phone went off. He didn't get many calls, after hours, so his digging-it-from-under-the-coat reflexes were not at their sharpest. When he looked at the screen, though, he immediately said, "Ah, it's Anna." His wife was instantly alert, abandoning her usual lake watching aspect.

"Hello, dear," he said. "I'd ask where you are, but perhaps that'd be violating security or something."

"Not at all, not now, anyway. I'm in the Capitol ... in the PR. We're on leave."

"Excellent. Just a moment ..." He looked around. No one was in listening distance except his wife. "Your mother's here. Let me turn up the speaker."

"Hello, Mother! I was just saying that I'm on vacation ... leave, you know. With a colleague."

"How nice," said Aoife. "So you've got someone to keep you company."

Anna paused just a second. "Yes, company." She pointed the phone camera at Siriom. "This is Siriom Barnes. We do a lot of our work as a team." Siriom managed to smile politely, rather than grin. "Hello. Pleased to meet you."

The call went on, covering things like comparative weather, a mention or two of relatives, the anticipated *what's-next* question. "We'll be going back up to the base soon, and then back ... out. On the ship, again."

Her mother tried to think of another thing to say besides *how nice* again. She came up with "Good, that's good. Isn't it, Stephen?"

"It's her job, after all. You mentioned, I think, that you'd found things?"

"Yes, yes, we did. Siriom and I ... " She paused. "We found an animal. A living one. And were going to try to write a joint thesis about it."

"Splendid, and ... oh, there's the rain, finally. It's been threatening ..."

"All right, we'll let you go, then. Don't catch cold. I'll call again, um, before we go back up."

"Very well. Thanks for calling." Doctor Grover closed the call. It was, actually, starting to rain. "Let's get in out of it, and then compare notes."

When the parents got back into the house, they spent a brief time taking off coats, putting on indoor shoes, and thinking. They sat down across from each other at the table.

"Well ... " said the father.

"Yes."

"You think so?"

"*Colleague?*"

"That was the term she used with that young man. You remember, last year. *This is my ... colleague.*"

"You're right. So, then. For my part, I'd just as soon."

Stephen picked up a glass of water, left over from dinner. "All things taken into account, I agree."

===

Eight: Finding a Thing

Siriom and Anna were finally back in the PR's 8th Division, experiencing a rather cold rain but a warm welcome from their colleagues. Out the briefing room window, Lake Gogebic was gray and kicking up a low chop. Now and then, you could hear a seagull scream at one of its kin.

"Welcome back." Doctor Greene was doing the mission kickoff as informally as always. "The really surprising thing is that we'll be going up to the Bolton, getting squared away, and shifting to another star system." No one said anything. "Now, I know that's really different ... no, wait, didn't we just do that?" She did get a laugh or two, that time.

DiBiasi spoke up. "Like last trip, we're going to the Scutum-Centaurus Arm. The planners liked what they saw from last time, and they want to see more of what's there. They've tasked us with six star systems, this trip, picked from the general survey plan. But they're all going to be new turf. Questions?" Nobody had any.

"All right, folks. Let's get geared up and ready to board ship."

===

Niels Untermann had come in to work quite early. His tests were nearly complete and ready to run, but there was another thing or two to finish. In very short order, the George Orwell would be in orbit and landing her crew. The software people would be going up, preparing to check and qualify the new installation. Niels would not be doing that, himself. He'd be here, preparing the install packages and posting them. They'd all passed their functional tests; the simulated Location shift engines had all responded properly. The software was ready to install.

At his workstation, Niels ran down the list of components to include. There were a hundred and seventy-eight modules, all assembled, compiled, tested, and ready to go up, digitally speaking, to the ship and into service. One of them was named *ShiftMode*. It was sixty-three lines of code, digitally signed and validated. He made a few modifications in his work environment, especially those involved in time-stamping files. Then he sat back and waited.

===

On board the Bolton, Greene called the science people together. They pulled themselves closer around her, holding onto grab handles. "Here we are, folks. At a brand new star - well, new to us. We don't know how old it really is, yet. Of course if it's *brand* new, well ... we'd be wasting time." Polite laughter. Her group liked her, and they put up with what was a fairly lame sense of humor. "There appear to be six planets hanging around. By luck of the draw, we've arrived sort of in the middle of things, planets-wise, and at first glance, number three looks kind of interesting. Anybody?"

Ari Pine, the meteorology lead, said "I'd vote for that. There are clouds visible, even from here." Greene looked around; no one else seemed to be voting, so she nodded.

"Good enough. I'll ask DiBiasi if we can nudge a little closer to it, and then let's get some orbiters down. Anna? Siriom? Carolyn? Steve? Any thoughts?" There were just nods and smiles. The hunt was on, and the hounds were tugging at the leashes.

===

This is an interesting planet, Anna thought. *This is one of the ones where you just want to be down there. Boots on the ground.* This third of six planets certainly had things that life-bearing space rocks needed to have in order to bear life. Its atmosphere was full of O_2 and N, *All that good stuff.* Anna tended to leave the gasses to the people who liked that sort of thing, but still those two made her sit up. *Air,* she thought. That's what I want to see. *If there's air, I'm there.* It was a basic requirement, not a conclusive one, but still.

The next good thing about this planet was that in addition to air, it had water. *Good old H_2O. Lots of it.* One of the first things you noticed as you entered orbit and turned on the sensors was that three quarters of the place was ocean. There was land, two continents worth, one at the "northern" end - from their perspective, anyway - and the other one straddling the equator. All the rest was a rolling, restless sea, drawn into massive surges and storms by its own rotation, that and the varying distance from its star and a single, rocky moon. Her colleagues were looking as far down into the water as they could, and Anna and Siriom were just beginning to get their probes and rovers in place.

The goal was to send surface assets down to places where living things might find other things to live on - for example, if there were plants, look around for things that might eat plants. Water is important; look near water. There weren't any apparent cities, but so far, there never had been any, anywhere. *Or jade idols.*

So far, the land looked pretty barren. Plant and animal life hadn't shown up in visible quantities, at least visible from orbit. Anna, Siriom and the rest of the Science crew had looked around quickly and decided to start surface work at a pair of separated areas. Siriom was taking one in the middle of the central land mass. Anna was setting up to visit a shore line where that land mass, - *call it a continent, if you want* - met the ocean. It caught Anna's eye because of its apparently abrupt transition. There seemed to be no beaches, no swamps, no river mouths - no rivers anywhere, in fact, and certainly none where she was looking. The land ran up to the sea and stopped.

Now, with orbiters in place, you could tell that it wasn't an extremely interesting choice. The abruptness of the dividing line between sea and shore was due to the land ending in extremely high cliffs. It varied somewhat, north to south, but the average was three hundred and ten meters of what looked like conglomerate rock rising up from the water level. Below, the ocean surface showed nothing particularly different from any deep body of water interacting with cliffs. Waves were hitting and rebounding from the cliff faces, yet the land at the top of those cliffs was still the dry, rocky surface that appeared elsewhere. *This is going to be interesting.* Anna spoke in the general direction of a microphone on the desk. "Launch room?" A voice said "Yeah?"

"I've got a probe and a rover ready to go. Can we launch?"

"Hold on ... which tubes?"

"Just tube four and twelve."

"Okay. Firing ... orange lights came on. "Done."

"Thanks, Aime. I'll have more later, but that's good for now."

As the gear descended, Anna switched to Siriom's orbiter, the one looking at the center of the continent. There had been momentary excitement over long, linear features, of course making humans think "roads!" Once the orbital device was in position, though, it became clear that they were old stream or river beds, showing signs of on-going wind erosion but with no suggestion of recent water flow. "At some point, there was surface water here, but no evidence so far of any at this point." That was the geologists' verdict.

And no vegetation, either, Siriom thought. Along those river beds was where it would be if there were any. Probably. You always had to say that. Every time you tried to generalize about a new planet, you'd get tripped up by some non-Earth-like phenomenon you hadn't thought of. *We've been here, what, three days? We don't even know if it has seasons.*

Siriom had pointed her gear at the inland area, at a point where one of the large stream beds originated. She had another pair aimed at a point where the feature just seemed to fade out. The geology people would be interested in that kind of data, and she hoped to find or rule out living or previously living things along what might be or have been a water source. Anna's idea was to land along the top of the cliffs she'd picked and go out to the cliff edges. As she unbuckled from her work station, preparing to meet Siriom for a meal, a thought appeared. Do we have any weather data, yet? That could be important, both for secure device landings and for the device's survival. *I'll ask Andy.*

Andy's team was exometerology, and its unofficial slogan was *Does it rain, and if so, what?* When Anna was doing her deployment planning, he'd advised her of potential weather dangers, to the extent that they knew of any. Sand storms or winds high enough to blow rocks around were concerns because they could damage lenses on the rovers; precipitation was an issue if it meant flooding that could carry the rovers away, bury them, or submerge them. Snow or ice, they could manage as long as their tiny reactors could hold on and melt themselves clear. She hadn't had those problems, yet, and she wanted to keep it that way.

She and Siriom ate, then came back together to the monitoring room. Anna saw the Weather Team's official status: *no idea yet.* Whatever kind of severe events the planet might experience, none had yet been observed. Andy had said his personal guess was wind storms, if anything, generated by ... a long set of meteorological terms that boiled down to *Wind. It could get windy.*

This didn't especially concern Anna. Flinging small, expensive things at the surface of an essentially unknown planet carried risks, at least for the things, and the Science crew's work involved taking those risks over and over. Obviously, it wasn't a physical risk for the people. The rovers went down there, and if one broke and stopped sending data, the team might or might not send another one, but it was an academic and financial issue, not a physical one. Every time she had one launched, she overtly wiped the cost from her mind. *For this thou wert born,* she thought, misquoting a misquotation.

While the gear was descending, Anna began to see data and

images for those western cliffs. Because of the probes' targeting, one of the orbital imaging satellites had given its attention to the cliff area, and when the first measurements arrived on Anna's screen, her response was a blend of concern and excitement. The concern was due to some unexpectedly extreme vertical dimensions; the cliff tops she'd picked were, on average, five hundred and fifty meters above sea level, higher than the run of the mill. *Straight down. Keep back from the edges.* She switched off all automatic movement instructions; when the rover was on the ground, she'd take it on little trips around the areas, but under her direct control and watched carefully from the probe. *No random movement patterns yet*; she'd set the boundaries for that, one by one, after personal investigation.

On the other hand, the surface area she'd selected wasn't just flat sand, running up to a cliff edge. There were patterns in the sand, presumably due to wind action, and her rover was going to come down damn near on top of a semi-circular dune. If you were sufficiently optimistic, you might guess that it would offer some shelter from winds coming in off the ocean. That would be good for two reasons. It might be a place for a rover to hang out in bad weather. *And maybe something is already doing that.*

It took another twenty minutes or so for the rover to hit the dirt. While it descended, Anna kept an eye on the orbital imagery. One of the satellites was closely aligned with the cliff-side landing spot, and she switched the data structure of its imagery to high resolution. The curved-dune feature looked even more as it had before: a dune, formed into a semi-circle with its open side pointing inland. She left the camera aimed there and switched to another sky view, looking for a landing zone. In doing so, her point of view reached the cliff edge. Two things struck her. One, it was just as long a way down as she'd thought, and two, there was some wave action going on. She canted the viewer upward slightly, looking farther out over the water. There were waves coming in. She watched for a minute, then made a call. A colleague of Andy's responded.

"Meteorology. Hello, Anna."

"Hi, Phil. Want to take a look where Orbital 51 is looking, right now?"

"Ah. Okay. Wait just a ... minute. I'm seeing ... Oh. Yes. Right. There's some wind down there."

"Yeah. I'm looking down from the cliff top, above that location. I don't have wheels on the ground yet, but ... let me see if I can get the probe focused on some non-rock. Hmm. Nothing but sand and rock, lying there quietly. Don't know what the velocity is on the land surface."

"You're putting surface units down there?"

"In about five minutes, yes. That's the plan, anyway. On the cliff top. Not down at the shoreline. If there's anything there to put them on, even."

"Noted. We'll ... ah, keep you posted, I guess. I'll have one of our birds try to look further off shore. See if there's really anything, um, happening. Off shore, I mean."

A signal interrupted the conversation. Anna's rover was below the hundred meters mark, coming straight down. There was no lateral deviation reported, no vibration, nothing suggesting that it was descending through severe winds. "Okay, thanks," she said, switching her primary view to the rovers' downward camera.

The descents always seemed slow, right up the point where they seemed far too fast. In fact, the little landers were extremely good at getting down and onto the dirt safely. This one switched its camera views to lateral from downward-looking just as its legs hit the ground. There was a slight jiggle, then it settled. As usual, Anna set the top surface camera on a slow three hundred and sixty degree sweep.

Well, it's not the garden of Eden. The screen showed, in a north, east, south, west circle, just sand and some boulders. To the east, away from the cliff edge, there was the inside of the semi-circular "dune." To the west, using the cameras on the probe, there was a view of the ocean, looking many kilometers out onto the water, showing a few whitecaps. Anna left it stationary, hovering and looking at the rover.

Situation normal, and so far, not AFU, she thought. That was always an unlucky thing to think, and she immediately had reason to regret it. The communication screen lit up.

"Hey, Anna." It was Andy. "Phil asked me to call you."

"Oh." That didn't sound good.

"He's got stuff going on, off to the east. Maybe a storm. Coming up really fast."

"Yow," Anna said. "Bad stuff?"

"No idea yet. First storm we've seen here. Anyway, heads up. You might want to look for some cover for the rovers - at least the one on the cliff. Where's Siriom's?"

"Way inland, ... but check with her, see if she's seeing any of the wind."

"Okay. Whatever's coming shouldn't be a problem there, at least. Yet."

Anna brought the probe over the edge, then switched to its rear-facing cameras. The ground was a combination of sand and bare rock. Bare rock could suggest that this area got wind, sometimes, blowing the sand away. That there was sand in other places could mean that fresh supplies arrived periodically, before being blown away. *And then, that dune. Is it a dune?*

She woke the rover up, pointed it at the cliff edge, and sent it forward. As it came alongside the dune, she stopped it and began zooming its close-image camera in. *Wrong again, Grover.* It wasn't a sand feature, it was a rock, and a rock with a very smooth, shiny surface, at least the one outside the curved wall. She spoke into her file. "Dune feature is actually a rock formation. Possibly sand-blasted by wind. Driving probe around it."

She moved the machine along the cliff side part, switching back and forth between front and side view angles. "Entire front of feature is smooth rock." She took a quick look behind the rover. "Rover's tracks in the surface sand will be wind-action indicator. If we get wind." If the wheel patterns blew away, that might support the sand blasting theory for the smooth rock surface. *Or, it could just be smooth rock.*

"Moving to the back side." She waited while the rover moved around the face of the feature. "Interior of the semi-circle is ..." She stopped the rover and had it poke one of its gripping arms into the sand. "... approximately six centimeters of sand. Rover arm indicates a hard surface below that. Moving rover away to clear for X,Y,Z measurements of the semi-circle."

She pulled the probe back inland sufficiently for the entire feature to appear in a measurement screen. A cursor allowed her to indicate left, right, and upper limits and come up with a 3-D model. "New rectangle upper left ..." A button click on the display. "Lower right ..." Another click. She pointed at the highest point of the curved wall. "Height ... " Click. "Map." The probe moved to a point directly over the dune - Anna was still thinking of it as a dune - and it began capturing a three-dimensional image.

As she watched, the image trembled slightly. A gust of sand blew up from the ground and dispersed. *Brief wind speed delta 0 meters per second to 4.* She turned on meteorology data collection for both of her units.

Siriom's voice in her headphones said "Are you getting some wind, out there?"

"Yes. Intermittent, just now. Giving ... hold on ... giving my probe permission to take altitude action." If the flier detected wind speed that would exceed its ability to hold an X,Y position, it would automatically move up, looking for calmer air. Another screen image jiggled. "And the rover is getting a push or two. Hang on, I'm sending this to Andy." She copied what she'd just written and pushed it to the meteorology people.

===

At the European Starbase, *Raumhaufen Clara Zetkin*, the acceptance tests showed a complete and successful replacement of the Location Shift software. With that, the new mission was approved. The George Orwell completed its gear and personnel verifications, ran through its departure and mission definition procedures, and shifted to its mission star. It sent one of its two un-crewed utility vessels - a small cargo and communication Starbot - back to the EU base. It delivered its message - "Successful shift to designated destination." - and shifted back to the Orwell again.

===

Storm was a polite term for what took place on Anna's cliff. She'd moved the rover around and into the stone semi-circle; she sent the probe flying off inland, with Siriom taking charge of it. The goal was to keep it from being damaged, if possible, and it seemed as though it could be. As the wind worked itself up, it appeared to be some kind of bi-level function. There was serious velocity from the ocean surface to the cliffs, but the impact with the literally vertical cliff faces seemed to be blocking the flow, slowing it down, shoving it upward in tumbling masses. It would have been hell for anything trying to fly in it, and things in the way of the fast, lower layer would have been overwhelmed - bashed against those three hundred-plus meters of granite cliffs.

As it was, each wave sent water - it *was* water, the team had determined - shooting up into the air and falling back, some into the ocean, some on the cliff tops. The semi-circle was quite wet, inside and out, and the sandy floor was turning into a watery mud. As the sand flowed away, the surface underneath showed itself to be more of the granite, the same material as the curved wall. She scanned the inside walls from time-to-time, for no particular reason. *No graffiti, no political slogans, no anti-litter messages ... what kind of national park is this?*

Doctor Greene pulled herself up to look at Anna's displays. "That ... rock ... was a lucky find. We'd be down a rover without it."

"True. Fluid-proof is one thing, getting rolled over and over and coated with sand is something else."

"Siriom is getting some hints of the weather, out where she is. But nothing like this. Those linear features are old stream beds. Probably very old. Just marks in the sand, now. So I assume these storms don't get far enough inland to interfere with 'em."

"Not, maybe, annually? Maybe it's been dry season, and now ... Whoa!" The rover moved on its suspension as a large amount of water came over the rock.

Greene shrugged. "Could be, could be. I'm a stranger here, myself."

===

On board the Orwell, the Science crew were looking over their new star's planets. There were only three, and the one located in the second orbital path seemed to be promising. The Starship commander directed the in-system techs to set up a local shift from their arrival point to a place within that second planet's orbit. The Starship, making use of the new, more precise location software, carried out an in-system shift to the new position.

===

With evening, the storm subsided. Anna stuck one of the rover's cameras up over the edge of its shelter. All it showed was the top of the cliffs and then a view far out to sea. There were still significant whitecaps, but it was apparent that the weather was through for the time being. *Let's see if we can get out of here. See if anything washed up.* The rover turned forty five degrees to its right, and she pointed a camera down in front. Then, she stopped everything. There was an object lying on the bare rock floor. It was six or seven centimeters long, a thin, gray rod, four or five millimeters across. There was a point on one end and a flat surface on the other. Anna blinked hard. *A nail!*

===

"Son of a bitch." MacIntyre wasn't in the habit of speaking out loud when alone, but frustration could override that practice. Today, he was annoyed because one of the people he'd assumed would be interested in his vague little communications hadn't been. In fact, that person hadn't acknowledged getting it, let along been encouraging. Also, he, MacIntyre, wasn't feeling up to par. He'd spent some amount of time in his sixties interacting with the health care system, and he'd then given it up as useless. *Not gonna step in that mess again*, he thought.

He made a cup of coffee, and walked out onto the porch. He was in time to shout at a family of raccoons who were hanging around. There wasn't any reason, really, why they shouldn't, but it was his damn property, after all. There was nothing handy to throw at them, so he just yelled. Eventually, they went away.

He went back inside and sat down at the desk. There wasn't any new email. "Dammit!" he said.

===

Even given the three-dimensional space around Anna's workstation, things were crowded. The *Virginia Bolton* was hovering on the edge of history. If the "nail" was what it looked like - an artifact made by a living species, not native to earth - the crew was experiencing the first human discovery of such a thing. And given that it had been found within a very short time of humanity's search for that sort of evidence, its implications for the rest of the galaxy were startling. "Our people have been out here poking around for two and half years, give or take," said Greene. "The odds are ... somebody else say it."

"There's probably more ... culture." said Captain DiBiasé. "Here or ... hell, anywhere. This planet, this system, or anywhere."

"Thank you. Now, the big questions. One, is it ... local? Or did we ... this sounds foolish ... drop it, ourselves, somehow?"

"No." Ashmet Geire spoke up. "Nothing comes onto this ship that I don't know about. And if it did, to get down there, it'd have to go on a probe or a rover. And it wasn't visible ..." She nodded at Anna "... in her footage until after the storm washed the sand away." The supply officer was known for her precision in ordering, loading, and dispensing gear. And a rover didn't have a place to stash things, anyway. It was a sealed box of technology with only its built-in equipment, no cargo space. And a probe could assess the stability of specific terrain, but it was by means of firing a projectile, not scattering bogus artifacts around. And beyond all of that, none of the activity connected with a Starship involved nails.

Siriom nodded. "I can't ... imagine ... it being anything but artifactual. I mean, left there, *dead and trodden to naught in the smoke-sodden tomb*."

"What?"

"Sorry, it's D.H. Lawrence. One of his grimmer poems."

"I'll take your word for it." Greene wasn't much of a poetry enthusiast. "So ... next steps. There is, in fact, a set of rules and protocols. I'll be going back over them in serious detail ... I mean, to make sure I don't forget anything. But the basics are, we transmit and record everything we can. Hands off, in the physical sense. We don't move things around." Anna nodded. "For a while, anyway, it'll be apparent that we were here. That the rover was, anyway. Tracks. But as soon as we get the full environmental data set from this area, we back the rover out of it and get a full inspection of the surroundings. Basically, finish the work that you planned, on this site." Anna nodded, again.

Greene went on. "One question we should try to answer - if we can - is whether the sheltered area was constructed. It doesn't seem like it, but we want to look at as much of it as is visible."

"We're going to do more surface work, though, aren't we?" Siriom looked a bit eager.

"Yes. As much of the planet as we can. But first, cover it from orbit. I want that to be an all-hands thing. Everybody who's able should be launching, controlling, reading data ... looking for anything that looks like a ... thing. Like this one." She pointed at the dune/rock. " Or anything else of interest. "

"One thing," DiBiasé said, "Should we try to get another ship here? To add to the gear and the analysis and all? Because the *Orwell* is out of the home system now, on its next mission. If we could get them to drop in, we could borrow at least some of their orbiters."

"Or get them to participate. I'll bet the Project would be fine with having two Starships on site. We could check each other's math, too."

"Yeah, right, right. Let's ask."

"We'll have to message back to Flynn base, then let them talk to Euro. I can get that started with Flynn."

===

Eden Gorsky, PhD in Economics from a US college whose name she had trouble remembering, General commanding the Peninsular Republic's Intelligence Branch, was capable of living that role. She did it quite well, in particular the being-imperturbable-and-calm parts. However, the message she was looking at caused her to draw in a sharp breath. It was from Meg Cordell.

"Sent 1510 EU time yesterday from unidentified individual source, private EU-spec comm device, to S339. "Goods delivered. Monitoring results.""

"Message originates in Starbase Clara Zetkin."

Oh, my. In the base. Better call Otto. Gorsky got O'Neill on the phone, catching him just as he was going to eat something -

whatever it was he had for lunch these days.

"Cordell's code picked up a call from someone at the EU Starbase. Some kind of goods were delivered somewhere, and the sender is monitoring results. Sender unknown, but it was sent to S339."

"I see. That's ... somewhat alarming."

"Right. And hideously ambiguous. The ominous thing about it is, *what goods*?"

O'Neill frowned. "The thought of additional funds comes immediately to mind. But also, explosives. I suppose that defines the extreme ends of a distribution. It would be nice to know who the sender is."

"It would. I'm sure Cordell is working on that, but I'll remind her."

"I won't say *keep me informed*, because that would be patronizing."

'And I won't say *likewise*, because I know you will."

===

MacIntyre usually got up at an early hour, then grabbed a nap after lunch. That nap was still going on when a message arrived. When he'd gotten up again, had a quick cup of coffee, and gone back to his desk, the message was waiting for him.

He read it. *Well, the computers guy did something. Be nice if I knew what. Doesn't really matter, I guess.* He made a few stock trades and sent one of his associates a veiled hint about another fund to consider. He got up from the desk, stretched, and went outside for a walk around the property.

===

Gorsky was watching the full EurAsiaNA committee meeting

with one eye on it and the other on a second screen full of budget data. Very little was accomplished in these top-level Starship gatherings; they were primarily for reporting on successful events, and most of the people attending knew about those events already.

This meeting presented the high level locations and status of the Starships. Bolton was on station at a promising planet and reporting what they believed to be an artifact of some kind. Orwell was on its first mission with the new software and was being instructed to leave its current star and assist Bolton with surveying its planet. The Heather Booth was in orbit over the EU base, completing its provisioning for a new mission and getting the new code.

"We expect the Orwell to operate with the Bolton for approximately one hundred fifty hours, and then to resume its itinerary. If there are important on-surface discoveries, we propose to task the Booth with taking on a targeted set of gear and science personnel and to assist Bolton with its investigations, allowing Orwell to continue its original set of missions."

Doing some ship swapping, Gorsky thought. *I wonder if they'll get The Bolton back here for the software update.*

===

"Captain, the base Starbot delivered a message for you."

Captain Maria Escobedo unholstered her phone. On a Starship, most messages showed up on something with a large screen, but the command traffic was available on a mobile device, too. She read the text, frowned, and called the science lead. After a short exchange with Doctor MacPhee, she sent a reply to the message, then another one to *all hands*.

"The Bolton has discovered what they are classifying as an apparent artifact, on a planet with water and an atmosphere. They have requested that Orwell move to their current star system and assist in a planetary survey. Please begin calling in orbiters and begin preparing to shift."

===

Nine: Days and Nights

Gorsky's phone went off. She didn't wake up instantly, but after the third alert, she opened her eyes. "What?" she said, quietly. Kristin was better at going to sleep and staying that way; she didn't react. *All right, all right.* Gorsky rolled on her side and fumbled for the device. She was familiar enough with the possibility of overnight crises that she kept it on the side of the bed table closest to the bed itself. The number calling was familiar, at least.

"Gorsky," she said.

"I'm sorry to disturb you, General. This is Caroline Bloom, Mister O'Neill's admin ..." There was an audible catch in the speaker's throat, something like a sob. "He's ... ill. Going to the hospital now. You were on a list ..." Another pause. "... of people to call." The woman had worked as O'Neill's assistant, door keeper, calendar guardian ... all of those indispensable things ... for as long as Gorsky had been aware of the man's existence.

"Oh ... no," was all she could come up with, initially. "Where ... are they taking him?"

"PR National. The ... emergency people called his doctor."

"All right. Have you called General Hallstatt?"

"No, but I will. You were first on the list."

===

The Republic was committed to an egalitarian approach to public service, but being one of the Army of the Republic's four Generals did tend to you get you past the healthcare system's call handling just a bit faster than if you weren't that thing. Still, it took twenty minutes to learn that O'Neill was receiving treatment for an ischemic stroke; that he had managed to call emergency services himself, but that he was now unconscious; and he was being given a plasminogen activator. The doctor was with him at that moment.

The person Gorsky was talking to didn't know whether there was a list of people to keep informed, and she transferred the call to Health Department Security. HDS quickly validated the calling number, noted that it was in fact General Eden Gorsky, Commander, Intelligence Branch calling, and they were able to tell her that she, General Phillip Hallstatt, and Caroline Bloom were the three people who the patient had named to receive information on his status.

By then, Kristin was awake and listening to Gorsky's half of the conversation. She waited for the call to end, then asked "O'Neill?"

"Stroke. They're working on him."

"Damn. That's ... potentially a disaster."

"Yes." Gorsky's phone went off again. This time, it was General Hallstatt.

===

One starship joining another was not a standard maneuver. It had been discussed. There was a draft protocol for it. But nobody had done it yet. *First*, Escobedo thought, *we define where we're going.* She started typing messages on her phone. The first was an acknowledgment of the order. It also asked for the Location shifter target information, pointing the Orwell at the Bolton's star. She sent that to her Starbot operator, with instructions to send it back to the EU starbase. Then she prepared another, asking for specifics of the Bolton's star and orbital location. That one was to be sent, obviously, to the Bolton. She also took a few notes for herself. *Start time, time to recover orbiters, time to receive and target the Bolton's location ... we'll want to do this again, and we might as well get a procedure in place.*

===

"All right, General. I'll wait to hear from you." Jack Severin was Gorsky's second in command. He'd been that for a decade. Along the way there'd been any number of critical conversations between the two of them, and the one just concluded had been one of those. It had to do with the potential loss of Otto O'Neill and with taking measures to manage other age-driven crises. Severin had confirmed something that both of them knew was coming, and he was relieved to have it out of the way. He felt bad for the General, though. She'd looked rough. As he closed her office door, she'd picked up her phone, and as he went back to his own place, he wasn't surprised that Meg Cordell passed him, going in the other direction.

Gorsky's admin waved her in. Meg wouldn't have used the adjective "rough" to describe the general, but "tired" came to mind. "Sad" as well.

"So, we've had some news this morning," Gorsky began. "O'Neill is out of the picture. Probably for good. He had a stroke."

"Oh, no." It was all Meg could come up with. She didn't know O'Neill particularly well, but she knew he was important. And someone Gorsky trusted. Highly.

"We're going to have to ... fill in some of the gaps, organizationally, and that's what I want to talk about. I spoke with Jack a few minutes ago, and I want to have pretty much the same conversation with you. This is strategic, not tactical." She took a sip of coffee.

"I've known O'Neill ... for decades. He and Doctor Klein had the idea for ... this." She waved a hand around. "The idea of a central intel function. I was running one of the Battalion groups, up in Seventh, and they had me come down here to help with a fraud thing that was going on. And then when I went back up north, first the trains stopped running. There was a blizzard building up. And then the Rainbow incident happened. O'Neill and Klein knew I was up there, one station stop short of the confrontation with those poor fools. They got me on the radio with a script and had me talk them down."

"I heard about that. I didn't know it was you, Sir. Talking to them."

"It wasn't fun. But we got 'em to give up. That was my first work with those two. Jeri Klein and Otto. She's been gone for a long time, and now Otto's out of service." She paused and looked away. "Excuse me." She ran her finger under one eye. "And then there was all that pointless nonsense down at Cub River. You were around for that."

"Yes. A bit of it."

"After that, Hallstatt and I had a talk. About how this job ... what we do, here ... was getting bigger. And that there wasn't any reason to think it would stop. So we cooked up the separate Intel Division idea. That's when you came in. And then, when Newhouse retired, and Hallstatt got her job ... poof! ... We're a Branch, all by ourselves. And a branch gets run by a General. So ... poof! ... Gorsky's a General. I didn't expect any of that. But ... *Safety and Comfort*. People thought I could do something. So I tried."

"Is there something *I* should try, Sir?"

"Yes, please. I talked to Jack about careers, just now. I've known for a while that he wanted to retire, but it wasn't definite. Now it is. He's not quite ready, yet, but he doesn't want to be considered as next in line. If I'm not here."

"I see."

"I want to give you a Major's badge and start showing you the admin side of this place. If something happens with me, you'd get the job. Hallstatt says it'd be Colonel first, with the General slot left open. And then, that."

"I ... but ... when?"

"No idea. I'm not going anywhere, voluntarily, for ... let's be realistic, four or five years. But it'll happen. And ... well, *O'Neill* ... he never said anything about his health, about retiring, nothing. Nothing about who comes after. I don't want to leave this shop ... to drift ... like that."

Meg looked away. "I think ..." Then, as it did when she'd made a decision, her expression hardened. Their eyes locked, and she said, "Yes, Sir. How do we start?"

===

"Are we complete? With the orbiters?" Escobedo liked to hear confirmations of things, even though she knew them already. She'd retired from the navy of a European Union member nation, then accepted this position because it was fascinating. Having both military people and academics working together wasn't all that much of a change - her last command had been an oceanic research vessel - and she'd toned down her military jargon and fondness for acronyms. But *confirmation* was still a thing with her. Now, she received it, with reference to the orbiters being recovered. She turned to the Science lead, Doctor MacPhee. "Ready when you are."

"We're set. Let's drop in on the Bolton." MacPhee was not military, in any sense, but he also appreciated the historic nature of this first-ever rendezvous with another Starship. "Tell 'em help is on the way."

"Prepare to shift." Escobedo's phone confirmed that they were prepared.

"Execute." Seconds went by. "Confirm order to shift," she said.

"Received, Sir ... it's ... the location shift is unconfirmed." On the Shift engine's control panel, the light under the *Standby* label was bright yellow. *Off, Operating*, and *Error* were all dark.

===

On Earth, in the Republic's Capital, in what used to be a university admin building, people's phones began to go off. Gorsky's was among the first of them. In about another fifteen minutes, she and Cordell were on a call with people from both the Starbases. *What was that thing? Something about never raining ...?* It wasn't completely clear what the emergency was, yet, but it was clearly an emergency. One of the more analytic members of the Program Group was trying to sum things up.

"What we know, empirically, is this." Pierre Solomé was speaking in French, but the translation algorithms were having no real trouble keeping up with him. "First, the George Orwell Starship has lost its ability to move. Next, they have enabled their backup Shifting Unit, and it is also non functional. Third, they can communicate ... their Starbot communication vessels work. If not, we wouldn't know about this, of course. Fourth, I suggest that we must examine these possible responses." He displayed a list.

"First, define the issue. Confirm that the problem is with the Shifting Units. Next, confirm that the Orwell can receive our Starbots as well as recovering their own. That is done - they can. Next, confirm that the Bolton is not experiencing such issues. Done - they are not. And attempt to diagnose the issue with Orwell's Shifting Units. Nothing has been learned so far."

"Second, we must choose a response. We could place the Booth in service as quickly as possible and use it in recovery. Or, we can instruct the Bolton to shift to Orwell's location, and use it to lend assistance."

"Third, we replace or repair the Orwell's Shifting Units, and return ship and crew to Starbase Zetkin. And uninstall the new software from any Shifting Units in service, and test all to insure function."

Gorsky muted herself. "What about that last one, Meg? We know the Bolton doesn't have the update. The Booth is at the base, probably getting it, or scheduled to. They can stop that or undo it, right?"

"Yes, sir, they can. But it seems as though we have to confirm they can send help. If the Bolton is down too, well ... it's all on the third ship. So it has to be tested. To be sure it's with the old software." She stopped; someone on the call was making a point of some kind. They listened for a minute, then Meg went on.

"I'm thinking of that last message we got, listening in on S339. *Goods delivered ...*" he made some calls afterward, just in the US, but *right* afterward. Financial things."

"What are you thinking?"

"What if the goods were corrupted software?"

"Oh. I see. Ah ... hold on." She turned the microphone back on. "Excuse me, This is Gorsky. Captain Cordell is with me, too. She has a suggestion. Captain?"

Cordell leaned in toward the microphone. "I would recommend ... strongly recommend ... that the installation release of the software be compared with the master files. At the binary level. Ensure ... that they match. I'd do that now ... do it as soon as possible." She typed a note on her pad and showed it to Gorsky. *Ask the US to talk to S339?*

===

Captain DiBiasi pulled himself up to Greene's workstation. "Something's happening. Orwell can't shift. Got a shuttle comm from the base. They want the version information for all of our Location shift software. Like, right now."

"Both the shift units?"

"Yeah. In-service and spare. No detail about the Orwell. Just *check the versions.*"

"But we know about ours, don't we? There's an upgrade, I heard, but we haven't been home to get it. Or can they do it remotely?"

"No. Everything has to come down, do the install, test it ... all that. So ours is going to be the same as it was when the ship was commissioned."

"And we're sure?"

"Yeah. The engine guys see the version number every time they log in. But they want us to confirm it ... I'm guessing they'll want us to go where the Orwell is. Give 'em our spare."

"Wow. *Okay, then.*" Greene started to type a message. "I'll let my folks know. They're going to be ... unhappy."

===

Meg and Larry were having a quick breakfast. She was going into the office immediately afterward, looking frequently at her phone. Larry had been concerned for a few days; she was being somewhat remote, somewhat more often than usual, and they'd been together long enough for him to guess that the cause was a professional issue. As she stood up, he asked an overtly casual question. "How are things in the shop? You seem ... busy."

She started to say something like *oh, they're fine,* but stopped. "Well ... "

"You're about to say "I can't go into details, but ...""

"No, not really. I can go into some of the details, with you, anyway. You can't say anything, of course."

"Of course."

"General Gorsky wants to move me up to Major. As a start on ... eventually ... making me the next head. Of the whole Branch."

Larry did manage to hold onto his coffee cup. He opened his mouth, then closed it again. He nodded, swallowed, and then said "Oh. Well ... good. That's good. Right?"

"Yes ... I think so. I can only think of ... two things that I really,

really enjoy. You and my job."

===

Docteur Pierre Solomé was in his element. In the last two hours, he'd become the de facto lead for this crisis, and despite his concerns, he was always glad of an audience and a chance to employ deductive reasoning. "We know, to this moment, that neither of the Orwell's Location Shift units is capable of shifting location. There is no error indication, it is simply that nothing happens." There were a few nods.

"As of ten minutes ago, we also know that the Heather Booth is in the midst of upgrading to the new software, and that the process has been stopped. However, the Booth is immobile. This means that we cannot send her to the aid of the Orwell. Soon." He paused. "But, we have just heard that the Virginia Bolton does not appear to have the new ... codes ... the software ... applied. And so, I conclude that the only reasonable course for us is to send La Bolton to the aid of Le Orwell."

"But, Pierre, " said a colleague. "Does the Bolton have spares? Or an ability to share the software?"

"All the Starships have a spare moteur. Naturally, after installing one of Bolton's moteurs in the Orwell, both ships would return immediately to their respective bases. They would not risk remaining out-système with only single moteurs."

"Docteur Solomé, I follow your reasoning. But there are issues." Gorsky and Meg were passing hand-written notes back and forth madly. "What if Bolton is somehow crippled, too? Software or no software? And if Bolton does get there, do we know that Orwell's people can do an install and replace? Or the Bolton's people, for that matter?"

"I anticipate you. I have just now sent that question ... the degree of difficulty of replacing ... to the technical people, and ... Ah, here is a reply. It says *engineering crews have training in unit replacement."*

Another committee member asked "Can we test the Bolton, though? First?"

"But how would we do that? By moving it somewhere? That is what they will be doing. They will be moving to the Orwell's location. If they cannot ... then we must put the Booth back in service as quickly as we can, load it with new shift engines, old software, both of those ... and rescue both crews."

"Just rescue the crews? Leave the ships where they are?"

"We would have to diagnose the problem here. The problem with the engines. And then go out to the two ships and fix them, bring them back. A much longer effort. And more expensive."

"All right, Doctor. Thoughts from others?"

Gorsky raised her hand, digitally. "Can we add a longer term set of tasks, things to consider when we're sure the crews are safe, that we know what the cause was, and so on? Setting up a kind of ... emergency group. Special ships, people, technology ... Aimed at reacting to things like this. And perhaps another group, charged with keeping this from happening in the first place?"

"That is exactly what is needed, yes, I agree. And I look to your people, especially, General ... that is, I would advocate strongly for that ... it would not be my authority to ... order it. And I would hope it could begin with the testing and approval. If we find that there has been an issue in ... them."

===

MacIntyre had been up and down most of the day, checking things on line, making a couple of largely useless calls, then lying down again. *Dammit, I'm gettin' old.* Finally, about four o'clock, he decided to have a sandwich or something. As he was putting it together, there was a beep. *Now, what in the hell's ... oh yeah, that.* It was a simple motion sensor he'd put in place, pointed at his driveway. He left the food where it was and went to look out the door. There were two cars in the drive. As he watched, two men in fairly ordinary suits got out of the first one. *Who ...?*

A relatively short time went by. Then one of the men in ordinary suits ran out of the house and moved the cars, one at a time, off the driveway and onto the lawn. A few minutes after that, an ambulance came up the road and turned in.

Not long after that, another of the ordinarily dressed men sent a message, presumably to his superiors:

"Contacted subject. Initially angry, then became incoherent, apparently suffered a medical emergency. Emergency Healthcare summoned. Subject was transported to a clinic in Douglasville. Declared deceased at 1750 hours this date, preliminary cause of death cardiac arrest."

Meg received a copy of that message, bounced from an agency in Canada. She showed it to Gorsky, whose response was "Oh, fabulous."

===

DiBiasi and Greene were together on the all-hands speaker net. "So, folks, here's the story," DiBiasi began. "Something's wrong with the Orwell. It can't move. The engineering people think it might be a problem with new software. They have it, we don't. And we're the only other one ... of the three ships, you know ... that hasn't been upgraded."

"Or downgraded," said Greene.

"Probably, yes. So, we get to location shift as close to the Orwell as we can, then pretend it's just like docking with the orbital shuttle. Seal up, pressurize both loading ports, swap the gear, and see what happens."

"Will we be coming back here, afterward?" Anna asked. "I hate to be ... selfish ... but we've got a kind of science crisis here, ourselves."

"Understood, Anna." Greene did, in fact, understand. "But we're it. It's a moose drill. We're the only ship that can get to them quickly. The Heather Booth is at the EU base, undoing its software upgrade. And beside just getting the Orwell out of trouble, they're nervous about ships being out here with a single engine. As we'll be."

"Right," said DiBiasi. "And I'm a bit concerned with that, too. Anyway, it's an order, and an order is, you know, an order."

Until one is strong enough to disobey, Siriom thought. She had been, in her youth, yet another person who'd read Kipling. "One thing," she said. "I have a suggestion for a star name. Here, I mean. NeoPossibilidades."

===

People came into the conference call and people left, essentially driven by external things they needed to do. One of them was just a messenger, really, with an update on the software crew. "According to the security people," she said, "all the engineering people involved are at work, today. Working on the Booth. Except two. A Monsieur Untermann and a Madame Bergé." She backed out and closed the door.

"Untermann? Why is that name familiar?" The software team representative wasn't a happy person. The longer this whole thing went on, the clearer it became that software was at least the heart if not the whole of the problem.

By now, Meg was overtly on the call and a de facto part of the group. "Wasn't there something about a man with that name? Something about ... quality assurance?"

"Yes. There was an issue ... a personnel issue. And he was reassigned to the testing group. He was a developer."

"On the engine upgrade?"

"Yes."

Gorsky had just returned from taking another call. "I remember that. Do we know why he's not at work?"

"There was, I am assured, General, a call for all the engineers to be here."

"Can we check? Did he call in sick? Go on vacation? Something like that?"

"Yes, we can do that."

"What about the other person? Bergé?"

Solomé looked up from his screen. "I can address that. Madame Bergé went into labor, just this morning. She and her husband are friends of mine."

===

"Now, go easy, there. That's not plumbing. Those connectors need tender, loving care." The engineering chief on the Bolton was mildly concerned. He'd seen shift engines installed and uninstalled, but he'd never managed the process, himself. "Last thing we want to do is give 'em something all beat-up." His phone sounded. "Yes, sir?"

DiBiasi was personally coordinating the physical work. He'd quietly promised himself that if anyone fouled up, it was going to be a thing for which *he'd* take responsibility. *This is above everybody's badge level, here. It's on me if we get it wrong.*

"How are we doing, Mike?"

"We've just about got it, Sir. It's like somebody thought this might happen. It'll fit through the door, out into the cargo hold. And the loading port's ready."

"Great. Here's a really stupid question. Have we ever docked with another Starship? Or just with the surface shuttle?"

"That's a *good* question, actually. We did it once, with the Booth. Training. It took a couple if tries, but we got it done."

"All right. Let me know when you're buttoned up, and we'll shift."

===

On the Orwell, Captain Escobedo, Doctor MacPhee, and Lieutenant Alicia Reeves were in the depths of planning. Reeves was the ship's Engineering officer.

"Right now, it's stand by to wait, basically. Bolton'll be getting their spare engine unhooked and ready to hand off to us. We've got our primary unplugged and moved away. The touchy part will be bringin' the ships together and locking 'em together."

"Right." Escobedo was worried about the positioning, too. "We can tweak our position a bit with gas jets, but Bolton's got to get here and get close enough for the algorithm to take over."

MacPhee's eyes opened wide. "What algorithm?"

"You know, the ... " Reeves stopped. "The code. That ... moves the ships together. Controls it."

"*Code*. I have to ask ... do we know if it's part of this ... failure?" Captain Escobedo didn't really turn pale, ever, thanks to her genome, but she might have.

"I will check that. Right now."

===

The conference calls were more or less perpetual at this point. Gorsky had stepped out, electronically, to handle some of the things that an Intelligence Branch commander had to do: briefing her superior, General Hallstatt; talking to a nervous Council Member; checking and initialing performance reviews; and refilling her coffee cup. Meg Cordell, on the other hand, had taken up residence in the Department's primary secure area. She was listening to a somewhat academic discussion of software quality measures; Gorsky came back on the call.

"This is Gorsky," she said. "I'm back." Her name appeared on the attendees list.

"Very good, General." Solomé looked a bit less like a diplomat. He'd unbuttoned his jacket, for example. "The ships have been instructed, and both are preparing to carry out the program as we have described it. The Orwell had a technical question, but it is being addressed by the Engineering people here."

"All right. Have we looked into that missing individual? From the ... what was it, Meg? ... testing group?"

Meg nodded. "He's being .... looked for. He didn't report in when they sent the all-hands message, and base security is trying to contact him."

"Yes, and they have also the Police Fédérale assisting them. There is no accusation, yet, but the ... what is it? ... *coincidence*, of a testing engineer being missing is ... suspect. They say."

"Ah," Gorsky said. "Well, looking at what Doctor Solomé has described, I think we should go ahead with it. Sending Bolton."

One of the US people frowned. "I agree, in the near term. But it seems ... tactical."

"Yes, because what we have right now *is* a tactical problem. The strategic problem involves things like background checks, oversight on critical tasks, new-release testing, well-defined lines of responsibility ... you know, business things, not search-and-rescue. SAR is tactical, where I come from."

"I agree," Solomé said. And he thought, without saying anything more, *I like this socialist soldier.*

===

There was some rapid movement of UUVs, back and forth from

the European Starship Facility. On both the Orwell and the Bolton there were sighs of relief. "No," said the Base Engineering teams, "Naturally, the docking system is completely different from the Location shift application. It makes no reference to star positions, masses, anything else, in fact, beyond the detectable signals from the vessels in question. The two ships attempting to dock. You understand." Even across the Galaxy, the somewhat patronizing tone could be felt. *How could you not know that?*

Lieutenant Reeves extended the middle finger of her right hand, aiming in a symbolic direction, based on the relative positions of the Orwell and planet Earth. "Code this, eh?."

===

"Alright, folks. Shifting in thirty seconds. Stand by." DiBiasi checked the controls one more time. "Okay, Reeves, let's go." They were with Location shift engine 1, and Reeves was at the keyboard. She typed "operate" and hit the *return* key. The Standby light went off, The *Operating* one blinked green three times ... and ... the screen displayed a few lines of coordinates, values, and statuses. "Worked," she said. "We're here."

For the next nineteen hours, give or take, they moved in increasingly smaller shifts toward Orwell's location. It was something like maneuvering a tow truck around a huge, almost empty parking lot. It was a three-dimensional parking lot, but the task was the same: get the vehicle near another one, but avoid running into it. After the first four hours, the Starships were able to identify each other. Since only one of them could move, the other had to creep up slowly, one short jump at a time. In order to connect, both vessels had to be close enough that one's docking system could sense the other's. When that point was reached, Reeves called DiBiasi.

"Docking's connected." There was a pause. "Sir ...? We're in docking range."

"Sorry, Reeves. Nodded out, there. Are we talking to them?"

"Yes, Sir. Here they are. Hey, Orwell, I've got our Captain here."

"This is Escobedo. We're ready to enable our docking signals."

"Acknowledged. Start 'em up, Reeves."

"Do, it, Taylor." One of Reeves' team typed instructions on a separate device.

"Signals operating ... contact ... good to enter docking mode."

DiBiasi looked around. Greene was with him, most of the engineering and science people were floating around in various places. It wasn't something you wanted to sleep through. "Do it," he said.

===

Around the edges of each Starship's loading port, there were sender/receivers - "SRs". Their function was to reach out to a similar set of devices on another ship, transmit their three-dimensional location data, and then include their assessment of the other vessel's values. The assumption was that only one ship would be moving, closing on the other one. Each set of each SR's data would be matched with the values the other ship was measuring. That one would correct its perception of reality, match it with its own previous values, and do a comparison. As long as the results were within tolerances, the approach would go on, flinging data back and forth. It there was a single large deviation or a set of smaller ones, things would come to a halt, and humans would have to intervene.

This was all necessary, since anything more than a very small deviation would, if ignored, result in an unplanned interaction. If it was at least harmless - for example, missing the other ship completely - it would be embarrassing but not a disaster. If it was less than an complete miss, well ... that would be a whole new emergency.

The good news was that base-shuttle-to-Starship docking took place on a routine basis. It had to. That was how crews and gear got back and forth between a Starbase and a Starship. But this wasn't quite that situation. Earth-Orbit-Only vessels were intentionally similar to their Star-going cousins, but still ... there was some concern. Anything one didn't do often ... something that could be disastrous ... well, there was some concern.

The propulsion for the moving ship was not a Location shift, not a jump through through the Universe. It was a very old and mundane method, expelling compressed gasses from one end of the the vessel, making it move in the other direction. Each one of the SRs on the moving ship connected with a pair of nozzles, each one able to generate velocity in one of two opposed vectors - backward and forward. Those vectors were relative to their specific SR, making the combined action of all the units steer the ship with a great deal of precision. The downside of that was that it was agonizingly slow to experience, watching displays as the distance slowly dropped. "Under one kilometer," Reeves reported. "Alignment nominal."

===

"Gosh, this is fun," Greene said. DiBiasi was with the docking crew, below. The Science people, having nothing at all to do with the process, were gathered on the top deck with Greene, watching the show.

"One K ... I'm not seeing it yet." Siriom was glued to a screen, with Anna hanging above and sharing the view.

"I hope they're in the right solar system," said Anna.

"I hope *we* are."

Liam Lynch, the Bolton's IT lead, was nearby. "Don't worry. Almar'll be handling this, over there." He gestured in the direction where everyone hoped the Orwell was. "He's got a lot of time in."

===

Slowly, slowly, slowly the two Starships drew together. The imagery being displayed inside each of them was unencouraging, if only because all they could see was a blank wall with a large, square door in the center. Around the Bolton's doors, the little SRs were still venting small amounts of gas, correcting attitude in smaller and smaller increments. Abruptly, the squirting stopped, and green lights lit up, outlining the doors.

On the Bolton, Lynch said "Well, they they think we're on target." On the Orwell, Reeves said "Locked in, Sir." The blank walls got larger. A range of shock dampeners extended from the Bolton's cargo face.

"Twenty meters," said a speaker.

"Stand by for docking." Reeves was poised by the SR controls.

"We're there," DiBiasi said, just a little more loudly than he had to.

Inside the cargo holds, there was a kind of soft, squishing sound, as dampeners compressed. With the areas sealed off, you couldn't really have heard it, but if you'd been down there, there'd have been locks snapping into position and the last hiss as the ships sealed together. Green lights came on.

"I'll be damned. We did it," said Greene. Siriom made a small noise, basically "Eee!" Anna put her hand on her shoulder, squeezed lightly, and pulled it back.

On the Orwell's Engineering deck, Escobedo held out a hand to Almar. "You do nice work."

Almar shook the hand. "Piece of cake. Let's get that shifter in here, see if *it* works."

"You are such an optimist."

===

154

Regardless of whatever time it might have been elsewhere in the universe, it was 0830 hours in the Peninsular Republic. Consequently, the National Broadcasting System began its morning news program. It was called, remarkably enough, "The News."

"Good morning, and welcome to The News. I'm Steve Radice. Morning reminders include Counsel elections coming up soon. There are four open seats and at this point, seventeen candidates. Be sure to check this address ..." A governmental web site appeared. "... for candidate biographies and qualifications. The travel report says that if you're heading out to work or school, there are no urban tram line problems reported, and only normal traffic on major highways. Now, with our current top news story, here's Catherine McCray."

"We've received a release from the EuroAsiaNA press office regarding a problem with one of the Starships. The EV George Orwell reported that it had lost the ability to move or "shift" from one location to another, meaning that it was effectively stranded in another solar system. The press document didn't specify the cause, but it did stress that there was no danger to the crew." She paused, looking off camera. "Ah. All right." She turned back to her audience. "I'm informed just now that another Starship has been sent to join the Orwell and provide it with one of its engines ... Location shift engines, as they're called. EuroAsiaNA officials promise that they will provide on-going updates as the situation unfolds." The camera cut back to Radice.

"All right, and of course, we'll keep you apprised of any breaking news there. Now ..."

Gorsky switched away from the broadcast. One of Meg's team knocked on the open door. "General, they've got the engine on board the Orwell. They're installing it now. And Captain Cordell is watching traffic from Europe and Asia. The Belgian police are ... " Meg came up behind her.

"They're looking for that developer who's gone missing. Untermann.

The only delta in the code they've found so far is some test routine of his. Sorry, Sharon, I interrupted you."

"That's all right, Sir. I was just about to say the same thing."

Gorsky yawned. "I didn't sleep all that well. I'm about to listen to our friend Solomé. We'll see how they're tracking the missing guy. Oh, and if the swapped engine works." Meg held up her right hand, fingers crossed.

===

Docteur Solomé was himself quite tired. He hadn't been as tired as this since the early tests of Starship tech. Or the process of forming the EurAsiaNA governing body. Or the birth of his first child. *I am in the business of being tired* he thought. *However, others are as well*. Many of the people on the call did seem to be short some of their usual sleep.

"What, now, what do we know that we did not know the last time we met? Docteur Ricteur?"

"We know, sir, that the Bolton's... ah ... additional shift engine is in place on the Orwell. And from a message just several minutes ago, it is installed, powered, and appears to be in a nominal state. The two Starships are unconnected again. The Captain of the Orwell is requesting authorization to attempt a shift into Earth orbit."

"And if it works, they will be ... here? No?"

"Yes. If it does not, we will receive a message to that effect. And if that happens, I will recommend that we begin transferring the Orwell's crew to the Bolton.

"This is Gorsky. I have a question."

"Go ahead, General."

"What if the Orwell attempts to shift, vanishes from the area the Bolton can observe, but doesn't arrive back in Earth orbit? What if it shifts, but ... to somewhere else?"

"That would be very bad, but it still has its messenger vehicles. It could still communicate ... well ... it could in theory communicate. Depending on ..."

"On where it was." An older gentleman, faculty at the University of Padua, appeared on the screen. "Even the new software does not attempt to correct all errors."

"But *Professore*, that has been the ... ultra ... of the Engines throughout. There is an infinite number of *locations*. All of the science ... everything ... depends on specifying *where* the shift goes. If that has failed ... what is the phrase? ... Cry havoc and unleash the ... animals of war?"

"Dogs," said Gorsky. "Unleash the dogs."

===

The day wore on, regardless of where you were. In the Republic, it was approaching noon. In Belgium, evening was falling. Aboard the Orwell, it was time for one of the meals. Captain Escobedo ate, buckled to a wall, talking to the Engineering officer. Neither one was paying any attention to what they were eating. Both were going over the contingency plans, procedures for re-connecting to the Bolton, for transferring the Science team. Perhaps they'd send some of the crew home as well. That would be a problem; most of them would want to stay. Lieutenant Elxeberria opened his mouth to say something when the UCV arrival alert sounded.

"Well, they've made up their minds," Escobedo said.

===

Around the conference room, both physical and remote attendees sat in silence. Coffee and tea cups were scattered around tables and desks. One of the younger people set his phone down and looked around. "It's been" ... he looked at his wrist ... "half an hour. Should we send another message?" One or two people looked up. Solomé opened his mouth to speak. The central display screen lit up.

"Starship George Orwell reports arrival in orbit at EurAsiaNA *Raumhaufen Clara Zetkin.*"

"Starship Virginia Bolton reports arrival in orbit at EurAsiaNA *Starbase Elizabeth Flynn.*"

"Fabulous," said Gorsky, "Let's leash up the dogs."

===

On the Bolton, people were experiencing a range of emotions. DiBiasi was relieved; there was a component of impatience, mostly in the form *let's get the science folks back to that planet.* Doctor Greene was letting go of a serious self-control exercise, moving back toward anger at whatever the cause of this nonsense might have been, blended with a touch of *this doesn't look good for the program* anxiety. Siriom and Anna were blending professional emotion and personal emotion, ranging from anxiety over the near-term scientific work that lay ahead to *I guess we just outed ourselves.* And Lieutenant Reeves thought *I hope we can get down for a day or so. I could use a drink.*

===

The base personnel in Belgium were immediately on line with the Orwell. Their first message was abrupt: *Ensure that software on malfunctioning engine(s) is not modified or removed.* That was followed immediately with a second one. *Welcome Home!*

Berlin's international airport was no longer new, but it was still a reasonably modern facility. With the decline in tourism and a vast increase in digital contact, it was quietly downsizing when the epidemic occurred. Like most of its kind, it closed, but the group responsible for maintaining it did a better than average job of preparing for an eventual reopening.

Now, the facility was again in operation, offering mostly trans-continental flights - flights to Asia, Africa, and the Americas. At a particular gate, people were lining up for an India-bound aircraft. A young man approached the check-in desk and showed the scanner his passport. The device said, as it always did, *Thank you. One moment.* It also sent a message to a specific phone number. There was a brief pause, then it displayed *Verifying. Please wait.* As the passenger reacted to that, a hand was placed on his shoulder. He turned toward it. The hand was attached to a man in a *Bundespolizei* uniform, standing there with two colleagues. The man said, speaking in German, "Niels Untermann, please come with us."

Ten: A Gathering-Together

It was early morning in a room at the Peninsular Republic's National Hospital, a big Capitol healthcare center, where people went when they were very ill. The room was just becoming slightly lighted through the window curtains. A pair of eyes began to sense that light. Gradually, they formed an image of ... a round shape. They struggled for a moment and then came up with an approximate distance: one or two meters, give or take. The light improved slightly, and the image sharpened, showing the round shape centered on a white square peppered with small black dots. As the eyes kept on transmitting this image, firing it down a pair of optic nerves, the connected brain began to function. What had been just the electrical impulses started to become an image. After some number of minutes, context started to emerge. Other areas of the brain received the image and tried to compare it with stored values. Finally, Otto O'Neill realized that he was seeing something. After thirty seconds or so, he grasped its essential nature. It was a ceiling light, mounted in the middle of an acoustic tile.

===

Not long after that Gorsky was on her way back to the office, coffee thermos in hand. Her phone interrupted her calendar checking. Roughly three minutes later, she was able to manage a slight smile. Her first instinct was to call Kristin, but she waited. *Get into the office, see what's going on with the other crises, then call.*

Her first crisis update was from Meg Cordell. "First, the FBI says they can't connect S339 with any specific group, but that he was pitching bogus investment futures to some people. And they're talking, quietly, to those people. The next thing is, the German police got Untermann. He was about to take a flight to India. And he had a thousand Euros in cash."

"He's a cheap date. What's the going rate for sabotage, these days? Has to be more than that."

"They're working on him, and it sounds like he's going to cooperate. We should hear more on the call."

"Fine." Gorski said. "There's a bit of good news, here. O'Neill is awake, and he seems to be recognizing people. His speech is fouled up, though."

Meg frowned. "That's ... well, it's good that he's conscious. But ... "

"I know. I really don't think he'll be back, not ... I just can't imagine that brain fighting its way back to where it was. If he can just get to the point of being sarcastic about national crises again, I'll be happy."

"Do you want to bring anyone else into the Starbase call? They're going to want to release something, publicly."

Gorsky paused. "Let's get Sharon Garcia in on it. Can you brief her? Then she can take notes for Hallstatt, and I can be ready to modify my little bit, depending on how it goes. And you can actually participate in the meeting."

"Fine. I'll try not to commit us to war or anything."

Gorsky smiled. "Excellent. You're learning fast." *Sarcasm, already. She's growing into her responsibilities.*

===

Jail wasn't what Niels had imagined. There weren't bars, for one thing. The room was small, bare, and locked, but it seemed closer to school detention than prison. He knew by now what the police wanted to know, and he was waiting for some legal counseling. But there was a strong idea, gaining strength with every minute he sat there, that he would cooperate. The woman who'd talked him into this could look out for herself.

===

"Good morning, and welcome to The News. Let's go right to Catherine McCray with the latest on the Starship problem. Catherine?"

"Thank you, Steve. The news regarding the crisis with an immobilized Starship is essentially all good, today. The ship that's headquartered here in the Republic was able to join the disabled ship and provide its own spare Location shift engine. Both ships were then able to shift back to their bases, one here and one in Belgium. According to a release from the program's headquarters, the issue was with an update of software, and both the European based ships will be reverting to the old version until the issue is resolved."

"That's certainly good news, Sharon, and I believe there was something about a joint group to do additional quality assurance ...?"

"On new software releases, yes."

"Well, that's certainly reassuring. Moving on, the Department of Health says that the next round of Covid 43 vaccinations will be available starting next week. And we've just seen a report that the last of the antique cell phone satellites has finally been de-orbited."

===

The conference call with the EU group was slightly altered in spirit by the last twenty four hours. The successes in bringing the Orwell and the Bolton back home were gratifying, but public perception was worrisome. On one hand, though. they'd picked *a* right answer, if not the only one. Looked at another way, the whole thing should never have happened, and the omissions that caused it seemed, after the fact, to be trivial and avoidable, and to have been the EU's fault. And then there were the Americans and the PR people. At least the Americans seemed to be willing to step back, leave it as a thing for the EU group to work out ... but the software group from Starbase Clara Zetkin were wondering what the Republic's Intelligence General would have to say.

"And so," said Program Director Stephanie Leydon, making a

rare appearance at the discussion, we need to do several things. We know, I believe, *what* happened. The young man who has been apprehended has told us that. We need to determine *why*, and *who* the people are who encouraged him. That much seems obvious. But ..." She deployed the classic rhetorical move, a pregnant pause. "... we need to understand how the change went undetected. And whether there is a risk of future such ... things. I will leave it in the hands of this team to develop a course of action, designed to answer those questions and assign tasks to prevent similar crises. I would like to propose Doctor Solomé as the leader of this effort."

Oh, mon dieu, thought Solomé. In Gorsky's office, Lieutenant Sharon Garcia typed *Team tasked with figuring out mitigation. Doctor S. to lead.*

===

O'Neill had an extra pillow behind his head; he was in a position that you could call sitting up. He had a moderate headache, and he was holding quite still. However, he was experimenting with moving his eyes around.

A human being in a very white uniform came into view. "Mister O'Neill," it said, "You have a message from a person named Gorsky. It says *Don't worry. Be happy.* ... Did you understand that?" To his surprise, he was able to move his head up and down, once.

===

The meeting carried on. In fact, the people being the most critical of the software effort weren't the North Americans but the EU Science personnel and the Chinese representative. Meg had a few technical notes to contribute. Gorsky kept her head down until she was asked to comment. In about five minutes, she was.

"From our perspective, issues with science of any kind ... computer science or political or any other ... tend to have their roots in tradition and indirection. Tradition of the *this is how we always do it* kind and indirection in the form of unclear lines of control. Who does what, and who checks to see how it was done. If I were looking at an issue like this, within our own infrastructure, I'd start with a call to the University's Information Technology department." Meg suppressed a smile.

The software group's leader reacted. "General, are you suggesting that the software development be transferred to the Republic?"

"No."

"You're not?"

"No. Think back up the chains of management and of financing and of personnel ... The knowledge of the domain is there, with you. There's no knowledge base for the engines in the PR. Think of the language set, for one thing. The star engine code is in AnaKonda and CPrime. Ninety-some percent of the software developed in our shop is in Cpr7. And finance? Do you want to tell the Financial Group they have to start moving the software budget across the Atlantic? And People? Families? Nope, I'm not suggesting that at all."

"I... all right. But, what ..."

"I'm suggesting that the *process* used for the Starship software ... Location shifters and all ... receive a structured review. And ... this won't be popular with the financial people ... it should have a separate review and testing group, reporting up a different path than development. That's how we deal with it here." Meg pretended to be answering her phone, concealing a wry smile.

"A separate ... group?"

"Yes, there in Brussels. That's what I'd do. But all I'm able to do is recommend."

Solomé had been keeping his mouth shut. Now he saw an opening. "I must say, I hoped that our friends in the Republic would have some wisdom for us. I would like to ask Doctor Leydon if she has ... funding for such a study, that is, the review that the General has proposed. And advice on the ... the structure it would take."

"I would very much like to see a proposed budget for a review group. I think it will be welcomed by the program board." Sharon's note on this read "Program director approves review." Twenty minutes later, Gorsky got a short message from Doctor Leydon: *Thank you. Nicely done.* Leydon then sent another one, this time to Pierre Solomé. *I would like to task you with this new review group.*

===

In a closed meeting of the PR's Governing Council, one of the older and more respected members rose to speak.

"My friends, " she began, "this last week or so has caused me some concern, and I know that some of you have felt similar uncertainties. Looked at superficially, this ... problem ... seems to reveal dangerous levels of managerial inability, especially on the part of the European participants. And I understand that concern. But if you'll allow me, I'd like to share some of my usual musing and existential wanderings."

"To begin with, I suggest that human behavior is existentially useless, but that some things are less useless than other things. Space examination is at least a good outlet for the pathological human urge to expand, possess, repeat."

"To talk in any useful way about what we know and what we don't know, you have to accept that we *can* actually *know* things. If you don't accept that, there's no point in your continuing to listen to me. Are there any post-modernists here?" No one responded.

"We have not yet found any empirically convincing evidence. We don't *know* if we're alone or not. So far, there's just that one hint, the nail that one of the ships seems to have found. We're curious, but is there anyone else out there with the same curiosity? Doing the same kinds of poking around? Those are things we don't *know*. But the fact that we had to drop everything and go save at least face if not lives from the effects of a crime committed by an individual idiot, on behalf of another individual idiot, is nothing more than a really good example of why we should clean up our act, as we used to say when I was young. Just in case some other species comes poking around, looking at us. Right now, I would find that very embarrassing, and I'd love to have evidence to show the hypothetical other species that we're at least *trying* to expand our horizons and models."

There was a brief silence, then the usual, low volume, "yes, yes," noise that Council Members made to signify agreement.

===

Siriom closed the call and set her phone down. "Done," she said. Anna arched an eyebrow.

"Done?"

Well, I said that I'd tell my father I'm staying here, and that one of the reasons is ... an affair of the heart. With a person named Anna."

"Okay. And he said ...?"

"He said *All right*. And in effect, *Have a nice life*. I told you about him."

"You did. Well ... now for mine."

"What time of day is it, in Liscannor?"

"Getting on toward dinner." Anna picked up her phone.

This call took longer than Siriom's had. There were the usual greetings, then expressions of concern about the Orwell crisis, positive things about their Starship having saved the other one. At a pause, Anna said "There's something else we need to talk about."

The remainder of the discussion was cheerful, positive, focused on near-term goals, on the potential for a visit, one way or the other, and it ended with the parents making expressions of happiness for their happiness.

"That was great," Siriom said. Anna agreed, but with the usual reservations an adult child has about springing her decisions on her parents, without having sought the parents' prior input. "Yes, in general, it was great."

In the house in Liscannor, right across from the harbor and the bay, the dialog was a bit more analytical. The father said "You go first."

"No, you."

"All right. I'm sorry about the no-grandchildren part. Otherwise ..."

His wife's eyebrows went up. "What? You're sorry about it? Did *you* want any?"

"No. But I thought you might."

"I sell wine and talk politics. What in God's name do I want grandchildren for?"

===

"Long day, Gorsky. Long day." General Hallstatt was always less formal with his Intelligence Branch chief than with his other direct reports. General Kydo was almost all formality. She and Hallstatt had known each other for ages, and they'd been peers, initially. But as head of the Field Branch - the military - she valued protocol and hierarchy; Hallstatt accepted that as a price of her deep knowledge and experience. And the head of Security Branch, General Sarafina MacLeod, was the Republic's chief of police. She was less formal than Kydo, but without the long experience in running a Branch.

Gorski, on the other hand, had been through most of the Republic's adult crises, the things that came after its unprecedented birth. She'd been there in the Big Bay aftermath, jumped into the Rainbow incident, and been at the heart of the country's response to a shocking invasion, known as the Cub River incursion. The two of them shared those experiences and accepted as a given each other's absolute commitment to the Republic.

Now she said "Yes, it's been a little trying. All that translated meeting-speak tends to give me a headache."

"I bet. And speaking of headaches, we need to deal with O'Neill's ... ailment. Council said "plug that hole.""

"How do they feel about the Starship ... event?"

"Oh, yeah, plug that, too. Any thoughts?"

"Well, about the Starship group, we've got Doctor Leydon's approval, and I've had a word with Information Technology. They've got a professor who loves software processes, and QA, and all that. They'd be happy to introduce us to him."

"Good. I remember a prof of mine. He used to say that specifying procedures and processes was so, so much easier than actually doing anything that he wondered why anyone wanted to write code."

Gorsky smiled. "The Europeans could use some processes, no doubt about that." The smile vanished. "What about Otto?"

Hallstatt frowned. "Well, he's going to be in the hospital for a while. The good news is that if it gets to the point where he can go home, his Admin ... Caroline, is it? ... is willing to move in. Live in the house with him and look after him."

"She has a partner, though, doesn't she?"

"She does, and the partner is willing to go with her. He's actually a medical sergeant in Field Branch, so when he's not on duty, that's a first responder, right there in the house."

Gorski sighed. "Well ... poor Otto. He loved his privacy. At least it's Caroline. But it doesn't plug the hole."

"No. What if ... your group tried to model him? Come up with ... a job description or a mission statement or something? So we know what we need to replace, at least?"

"It'd be a highly-classified document, that's for sure. And we'd have to canvass a lot of departments besides just the Army. Anything in the way of a crisis used to come across his desk."

"I know." Hallstatt's expression changed from tired to quite tired. "Suppose we do it together? Keep the planning for it on my desk and yours? Oh, maybe bring your new Major ... did you do the promotion papers on her? ... into it, too?"

"I'll get the paperwork to you tomorrow. But, yeah, this would be good on-the-job training for her. Give her some insight into the dark side of the moon." Gorsky paused. "What did you make of that ... person in the US? S339?"

"From what I've heard, he was good at staying just on the edge of criminal. Just barely smart enough to keep his head down. Oh, and to stay out of crypto currency."

"I'll give him that." She frowned. "And then, there's ... the other thing."

"Right. Voldemort." There was, in fact, another term for Gorsky's allusion. Neither she nor Hallstatt used it outside class three secure rooms. She was in one, but he was only in his office. "Did Counsel agree on the high level objective?"

"By a small majority, yes. There are questions."

"I bet. Have you got time this week? It seems as though recent ... things ... might be relevant."

"I'll get Shelly to set up a time. When our class three is available." He paused. "Sorry, I have to take another call. Finance people want to talk about budgets."

"Enjoy." Gorski signed off, then leaned back, closing her eyes. "*What if ...*" she thought, imagining a future in which the primary direction of the Starship Counsel was defined by Chinese and PR experts, with the objective being to bring the now loose and distracted Asian participation into a multi-national alliance. And ... to begin quietly shifting leadership of the program away from the EU and toward groups that could at least spell socialism. *This latest little hiccup is ... an opening.*

===

Starbase Flynn was slightly chilly. There was a breeze blowing east across the lake, just hard enough to ripple the water. Siriom, Anna, and Doctor Greene were standing on a small wooden dock, south of the launch pad. Directly across the lake, you could see a break in the woods where a bridge crossed one of the swampy inlets.

Greene had brought a pair of binoculars; she had some small enthusiasm for bird watching. There were plenty of Canada geese to watch, but since you'd encounter them wandering around the Starbase itself, they weren't particularly exciting. She passed the glasses to Siriom. "Have a look. You could hide a whole civilization in all of that, over there." She waved her hand at the forest across the lake,

"Thanks." Siriom swept the binoculars north and then back south. She handed them to Anna. "I didn't see any jade idols."

Anna took them, then pointed them north, up the lake shore. "I think there's something ... up there. A clearing of some kind. Like a park. If it has idols, the cult probably isn't very affluent." Greene looked that way, too, then back at the speaker.

"We really are going back. To the nail planet."

"I know. It's ... when I'm working one of those sites ... on a planet, any of them ... I have a hard time sleeping. I just want to be back in front of the screen. Finding things."

"Me, too." Siriom was looking at the water, still.

"And it's the same, right now," Anna went on. "It's ... unfinished business. That's all."

Greene nodded. "We'll finish it. As far as we ever actually finish anything. Of course, you two have a thesis to finish. And ... some decisions." She looked at Siriom.

"Decisions. Well, I'm ... complete on that task. I want to stay." She reached out toward Anna. They stepped closer and joined hands.

"I see. Well ... " Greene paused a beat. "... good. I won't pretend to be surprised."

"We haven't really been very discreet, I suppose. But ... yes. We both want to stay." Anna was smiling in a way the research chief hadn't seen before.

"Good, good. I'm repeating myself, but ... good." She retrieved her binoculars. "Well, I've got to go back in, get some funding things worked out. See you at dinner."

The breeze shifted to the south, blowing down the lake. The sun was just setting over the trees on the far shore, glancing off ripples. A fragment of lyrics came to Anna's mind, something from a very old song. *Who was that? King Rouge, Prince Crimson? I called you lady of the dancing water ...* She looked at Siriom and smiled.

END

Afterword

<u>The Starships, Starbases, and Other Names That Appear</u>

Virginia Bolton	19th-20th century Argentine Feminist
George Orwell	20th century British Socialist Writer
Heather Booth	20th century American Feminist
Elizabeth Gurley Flynn	20th century American Labor Leader and Feminist
Clara Zetkin	19th-20th century German Socialist
Mary Harris Jones	19th-20th century Labor Organizer

From the author

This is the ninth novel I've written, all of them placing the primary characters and action in what is now, as I write this, the State of Michigan in the United States. The books are more like each other than they are different, sharing geography, several consistent characters; and the occasional bad joke.

You'll find bits of decor scattered around, mostly literary or musical references, and they reflect aspects of my personality, my tastes, and the situations I've stumbled into.

Books

<u>Stories and Poems</u>

With His Ship Intact

  The Run of Myself

<u>Mac MacArthur Novels</u>

Many Believable Lies   *Clash By Night*

The Least Weasel   *A Lair for the Wolves*

  Driven by the Trades

<u>Peninsular Republic Novels</u>

Dog Island   *The Stars Came Otherwise*

  A Fortnight in April   *Amid a Crowd of Stars*

These are all available from Amazon at:

https://www.amazon.com/stores/author/B00DQUQI16

as both Kindle e-books and paperbacks.

www.ingramcontent.com/pod-product-compliance
Lightning Source LLC
Chambersburg PA
CBHW072354190626
46811CB00019B/870